# Marcellinus:
## The Silk Road Warrior

by

Matthew Rodriguez

authorHOUSE®

*AuthorHouse™*
*1663 Liberty Drive, Suite 200*
*Bloomington, IN 47403*
*www.authorhouse.com*
*Phone: 1-800-839-8640*

*First published by AuthorHouse 1/6/2009*

*ISBN: 978-1-4389-0913-4 (sc)*

*Printed in the United States of America*
*Bloomington, Indiana*

*This book is printed on acid-free paper.*

# Table of Contents

# Chapter 1

Long ago, when the world was young, in a time of great adventures, when legends were born, in a world that was war-torn over territorial disputes and a rise of power, there was an untold legend of a man, a man who would help create a great historical passage from China to Syria. For history just speaks of Emperor Wu and General Zhang Qian and their efforts to create this road, but I do not speak of these two. No, I speak of the *real* inventor of this road, a man named Marcellinus.

The story begins in ancient China, circa 162 BC, in a time ruled by a powerful man, Emperor Jing. It was in the midst of the Han Dynasty, perhaps China's greatest empire of all time.

Close to the city of Chang'an, where Emperor Jing lived, was a small house on the banks of the Yellow River belonging to a middle-aged man named Hototo Takeshi. He was a very learned man, for he was a scholar. He had made many travels throughout his life and had seen many parts of China. He owned several different books on the many languages of the world, and he had learned them all, not to mention he was also a very skilled swordsman. Although he had a very successful life, he still felt empty. For even though he learned many things throughout his life, he never had the time to find a wife and have a family, which made Hototo very lonely.

On one night, in the middle of a terrible storm, the Yellow River was overflowing at an exceeding rate. Hototo was coming home late from an important meeting with one of his associates when he happened to see something oddly shaped floating down the river. Hototo couldn't see very well, so he slowly made his way closer, and as he got closer and closer, he started hearing the faint sound of crying. *A baby?* he thought. Quickly, Hototo picked up the object and noticed it was wrapped in many cloths and was in a small, but crude, wooden basket. He uncovered the top to discover the face of a small child. Without a second thought, Hototo made his way home as fast as he could. Once inside, he quickly dried off the soaking wet body of the helpless infant and made a shocking discovery. He noticed the infant was much paler than he, and his eyes were shaped very differently as well. Under the baby in the basket was a note written in a strange language. Hototo, being a scholar, almost immediately recognized the language. It was written in Latin. The letter was a bit smudged from water damage but it was still legible. The letter told the story of who this baby was and from where he came. "My name is Luna. I am wife of the great Lord Michaelanor. Due to unforeseen circumstances, my husband and I will be killed tonight by Roman legionnaires. We thought we could elude them by escaping to the city of Jinan, but to no avail. So I have put my son in this basket in the hopes he could have a future. His name is Marcellinus. Whoever is reading this, I implore you, please take care of my son. Signed, Lady Luna." Upon reading this letter, Hototo was at a loss for words. What should he do? Should he report this to the imperial guards? *No*, he thought, *they would only have him executed for being a foreign child.* Still unsure of what to do, Hototo looked at the child, and it started to give him a smile—a smile so strong it melted Hototo's heart just looking at it. At that moment, Hototo decided that keeping him as his son was the best thing to do, for he always wanted a family and now was his chance. He could give Marcellinus an excellent future, he thought.

Many years passed, and during those many years, Hototo had taught Marcellinus to speak and write Hanyu, Latin, Arabic, Norse, Japanese, and many other languages. Hototo also trained his brain, as well as his body, for three hours a day. He taught him to use swords, axes, arrows, knives, and spears. By the age of twenty, Marcellinus was an expert in language and fighting. He started working with his father, Hototo, as his apprentice. Every seven days they would visit the palace of the emperor to deliver news of the world and any herbs or weapons that they needed. Marcellinus would spend many hours forging powerful weapons for the emperor's army, but he never felt his father received enough coins for his effort or duties. However, Marcellinus was not one to disrespect the emperor or his father, so he continued to do as he was told. In these past twenty years, Marcellinus had grown to be an amazing man. He was not very tall, standing at about five feet and nine inches. He was quite muscular and had shoulder-length dark brown hair. He was also spouting a slight beard. As for Hototo, he had gotten much older these past years. He now had many wrinkles upon his brow and had an impressive beard that stretched past his chest. He also walked with a hunch and with the support of a cane. Both he and Marcellinus wore the traditional Zhiju and Putou hat that many scholars wore (which was a long white robe and a small, circular white cloth hat that sat on one's head like a kippah).

One day in 141 BC, something tragic occurred. Emperor Jing had passed away, leaving his son, Prince Che, to rule in his stead. Almost immediately, though, Che had changed his name to Emperor Wu. Hearing of this distressing news, Hototo decided to make his journey towards the palace to send his regards. Hototo had packed everything he needed, from herbs to spices and also the golden sword passed down from his father; he was to present it as a gift to Emperor Wu for Jing's memory. As they walked towards the palace, Marcellinus turned towards his father and said, "Father, are you sure you want to give Wu your family heirloom, the golden sword?"

Hototo looked at his son with shock and disbelief, "Of course I do, Marcellinus. The emperor is an important part of China. Without him, it would be in chaos. If this will help ease his suffering then so it shall be. Oh, and Marcellinus, you will show Emperor Wu respect by saying his title before his name. Understand?"

Marcellinus looked at his father proudly as he saw no one more dedicated to pleasing the royal family. "Yes, Father; my apologies."

Soon they reached the imperial palace, and it was even more beautiful each time they saw it. The surrounding town was bustling with much activity, and Marcellinus had never seen so many colorful Shenyi and Qujus before, which was the traditional outfit commoners wore (they were similar to robes and were usually red or blue). The buildings in the city were not as impressive as the actual palace; they were very similar to Hototo's house, made of stone with a bamboo roof. But the palace…the palace was very beautiful indeed. Silver, gold, jade, and ruby as far as the eye could see. Impressive golden statues and marble pillars blessed every pathway and doorway. Many imperial guards were also standing at attention in front of the palace, which many held the precious spears that Marcellinus himself had forged.

They finally reached the foot of the palace as the new Emperor Wu was coming forth. A guard shouted, "All hail Emperor Wu!" With that said, all guards and townsfolk, including Hototo and Marcellinus, bowed at his presence. Emperor Wu was a stout man, only standing a mere five feet and three inches. He wore a very fancy royal Mianfu outfit (which was similar to a fancy bathrobe ordained with an assortment of colors and sometimes flowers) and guan hat (which was worn like a kippah with a large flat surface on top in the shape of a rectangle). He had a long, pointy beard and a chubby face.

"Ah, Hototo and Marcellinus, what brings you here?"

Hototo raised his head and pulled out the golden sword and his bag of herbs and spices. "I have come delivering a present to your highness as both a welcome for becoming emperor and as a memento to your late father, Emperor Jing. I have also brought many herbs and spices as well."

Emperor Wu looked at the golden sword with disgust as if it were a cheap steel sword and said, "Humph. Though this sword is quite hideous, if it is really all you pathetic street urchins can afford, then very well; I might give it to my future son as a toy someday ha, ha, ha, ha!"

This made Marcellinus very angry. How dare this stuck-up piece of trash talk to his father that way. He quickly rose to his feet. "Wu! How dare you talk to my father like that! No one in this country respects and honors you more than him!"

At once, Emperor Wu became very angry as well. "Fool! How dare you talk to me like this, you foreign piece of trash. You are nothing but a Xirong (a common name given to most foreigners as a sign of disrespect)! Guards! Seize him!" At once,, about five guards confronted Marcellinus with spears in hand and grabbed him by the shoulders.

"Wait!" cried Hototo. "Please, my emperor, you must forgive him! He is but a foolish young man. He knows not what he says. On my honor, he shall be thoroughly punished once we get home."

The emperor, seeing a golden opportunity, looked at Hototo with a smirk. "Very well, Hototo, but as penance for this insolence, I want ten bags of coins."

Marcellinus, looking at Hototo with sadness, said, "No, Father, do not! That is all the money we have."

Hototo, without a second thought, agreed to the emperor's terms. "As you wish, your majesty."

Emperor Wu, with a big smile said, "Good, good. I will expect my coins in two days." With that said, the guards released Marcellinus, and Hototo bid the emperor farewell as the two made their journey back home.

As they neared their house, Marcellinus turned to his father with anger. "Father, how could you give that man all our coins?! What will we do for food and your medicine?"

Hototo just calmly said, "Well, Marcellinus, if it wasn't for your foolishness and lack of respect, we wouldn't be in this mess, now would we?"

Marcellinus looked down at the ground in shame. "Father, I am sorry…"

Hototo looked at his son with loving eyes, "It is all right, my son. I would rather give up all my money and my house than see you executed. I love you, my son, and nothing will ever change that." The two gave each other a loving hug.

"Father, I love you, too."

Two days later, Marcellinus prepared for his journey to deliver the coins to Emperor Wu. "Father! Are you almost ready? We should leave soon!" Marcellinus made his way to his father's bedroom only to see him still in bed and in very bad shape. Marcellinus was very worried. "Father! What's wrong? Are you okay?"

Hototo slowly moved his head towards Marcellinus. "No, my son, I have come down with a terrible illness. I…*cough*…can hardly move."

Marcellinus was very concerned. "What can I do, Father? We have no coins to buy any medicine."

Hototo just smiled. "Do not fear, my son. I will be fine. You must deliver the emperor his coins. Go now before it gets too late."

Marcellinus, with a tear in his eye, looked at his father, "Father do not worry. I will find a way to get your medicine." With that said, Marcellinus grabbed the bags of coins and started his journey towards the palace.

# Chapter 2

Marcellinus made his way to the palace and awaited Emperor Wu's arrival. As Emperor Wu emerged, he had one of his generals walking next to him. They were talking about something most interesting. Quietly, Marcellinus began to eavesdrop. "My lord, it is impossible to make a path from China to the foreign land of Europe. The pathways are filled with all sorts of incredible danger. None of my men or I would be crazy enough to partake in such a quest."

Emperor Wu looked dissatisfied. "If I cannot make a pathway to Europe then how will I ever hope to fulfill my dreams of trading silk?" Emperor Wu angrily grabbed the general. "I will not be denied my dreams because you and your men are too cowardly!"

The general, sweating profusely, nervously said, "B-but your highness, what can I do? None of my men want to go! Please have mercy. There is nothing I can do!"

The emperor then just dropped the pathetic excuse of a man. "Fine! If you cannot achieve this task then I will do something about it myself!"

Suddenly, one of the guards made an announcement. "All citizens report to Emperor Wu at once!"

After a while, the entire town was standing at the entrance to the palace. Emperor Wu then stepped forth. "Attention, my subjects! I, Emperor Wu, have a request to ask of you. I want to make a trading route from here to the West, to Syria, so we can share and trade our abundance of silk with the world. This will change our very way of life. This task will be extremely difficult, so as a reward I shall grant your deepest desires! So who here is man enough to partake in this quest?" Everyone was silent, for everyone knew of all the unsurpassable dangers the western lands held. There were stories of ruthless warriors, monsters, and demons, not to mention the dreaded Roman legionnaires.

One of the guards spoke. "Come on, you worthless people! It is for your emperor!" Still no one spoke a word.

Marcellinus then saw this as his greatest opportunity, for if he could create this passage of trade for Emperor Wu, then he could help his father get better again, not to mention they could live a better life in a bigger home. He quickly rose to his feet. "I will go."

Emperor Wu, surprised, looked at who said this, "You? Ha! You are just a Xirong! You could never do what I ask." All the villagers started laughing as well, believing Marcellinus to be a fool. Just then, Emperor Wu thought that sending Marcellinus to do this might not be such a bad idea, for there was no way he could do this task and would surely die. He would never have to see this Xirong's face disgracing the beauty of his city again. He spoke. "Very well, Marcellinus. I shall grant you permission to partake in this quest, and if you succeed, you shall be greatly rewarded. What would you like as a reward?"

All of a sudden, Emperor Wu's beautiful sister walked out of the palace. Her name was Princess Nangong. She was the most beautiful woman in all the land of China. She was about five feet and two inches tall. Her face was covered in glowing makeup with lips the color of roses, and her eyes shined like the beauty of a jade. Her green eyes were not her only unique feature, for she always wore the best clothing as well. Princess Nangong wore a semi-formal Quju with many flashing shades of blue and white, with an elaborate gold Ji hairpiece. "Ah…" Emperor Wu said with satisfaction. "I see you favor my sister Nangong. She is quite beautiful, is she not?"

Marcellinus, a bit embarrassed, answered, "Y-yes, your highness, she is indeed." Of course she was. Marcellinus had seen her since he was fifteen and had always admired her from afar.

Emperor Wu spoke. "I see. Well, Marcellinus, if you complete this task for me, then I shall grant you my sister's hand in marriage."

Everyone seemed shocked by this, Princess Nangong and Marcellinus especially. Marcellinus then hesitantly spoke, "Really? Oh, but I…"

Emperor Wu then snapped back, "Is my sister not good enough for you, Xirong?"

Marcellinus quickly responded, "Yes, of course she is, your highness! It is just that my father, Hototo, has fallen ill and is in need of medicine, so I was hoping my reward would also be a way to take care of my father."

Emperor Wu laughed. "Oh, well of course! I shall give you and Hototo a mountain of gold if you complete this task!"

Marcellinus was very happy. "Thank you, your majesty!"

Emperor Wu then looked towards his subjects. "Let it be known that I, Emperor Wu, have granted permission to this foreigner, Marcellinus, to partake in the perilous journey to and from the western lands so as to make the pathway safe for travel for all of time! And let it be known that I have promised him gold and, of course, my fair sister's hand in marriage!" With that said, the townspeople all cheered. "Now go," spoke Emperor Wu. "Go home and prepare for your journey and report back here at my palace when you have completed your journey. Oh, and do not forget to bring me back some sort of evidence proving that you really did indeed complete your journey."

Marcellinus looked at him. "Yes, of course, your majesty. I shall bring back a token of proof from the city of Syria."

Satisfied, Emperor Wu sent him off. "Very well; now go!"

Marcellinus then made his way back home after handing the bags of coins to a soldier on the front steps of the palace. As he left, both the general and Princess Nangong looked at Emperor Wu disgustedly. Princess Nangong was the first to speak. "Why did you promise that man my hand in marriage? I do not wish to marry him!"

Emperor Wu just smiled. "Oh come now, sister. I see the way you look at him. You know you like him. For five years now you have flirted with him."

Princess Nangong blushed. "No I have not! I cannot marry him. I am a princess. It is forbidden!"

Emperor Wu was a bit annoyed, "Calm down, Nangong! Do you really think that fool can achieve this task? If so, then you are a bigger fool than he!"

Princess Nangong then smiled and laughed. "No, I guess you're right, brother; he can never pull this off. He will die before he even reaches China's border." Then they both laughed as they walked back into the palace.

When Marcellinus returned home, he noticed his father standing outside, waiting for him. "Father!" he cried. "What are you doing out here? You should be inside, resting."

Hototo slowly spoke, "No, I am fine. How did it go?"

Marcellinus was a bit hesitant in telling his father the news, "Well, it went fine. I delivered the coins as promised."

Hototo looked pleased. "Good, good."

As Hototo was making his way back in, Marcellinus built up his courage and told his father the big news. "Father, I made a deal with Emperor Wu. If I travel to and from the city of Syria clearing a path for his trade route, he will give us a mountain of gold and Princess Nangong's hand in marriage."

Hototo was exceedingly shocked by this news, so much so that it seemed he was having a heart attack. "What? Marcellinus, is this true? Do you have any idea what kind of dangers await beyond the borders of this city?" Marcellinus said nothing and just looked down at the ground. "And marry Princess Nangong? She is royalty. We are not. It is forbidden!"

Marcellinus looked up. "Father, what I tell you is true. Emperor Wu made an official announcement to the entire city. You are not one to disobey imperial commands."

Hototo was upset but at a loss for words. "You are…you are right, Marcellinus. If Emperor Wu indeed said this, then you must follow orders."

Just then, a messenger from the palace arrived on horseback. "You there! Are you Hototo? I have a message from Emperor Wu!" After that, the messenger gave Hototo a scroll and rode back to the city. Hototo opened the scroll and read its contents. The scroll was an official proclamation of Marcellinus's journey. Now Hototo knew Marcellinus was telling the truth.

"I see." Said Hototo, "If you are to go on this journey, you must be prepared for it. Come inside." They both ventured indoors, and Hototo began to pull out many books. "The scroll says you must depart tomorrow, so we have many things to do before then."

Hototo began reviewing all the different languages and also made Marcellinus spar for many hours.

Later that evening, Marcellinus began to speak at dinner. "Father, I heard this path is filled with demons and monsters. Is that really true?"

Hototo looked troubled as he began to speak. "Yes, Marcellinus, it is indeed true. Throughout my travels to Lanzhou and back, which you know is the closet village to here, I've heard the villagers say many things while I was there. Now I did not stay long, and that is the farthest I have traveled, but I heard many villagers telling tragic tales of how they lost many loved ones to the dreaded Pangrandawu."

Marcellinus looked puzzled as he tried to figure out what this word meant. "Pangrandawu? The…the cyclops?" Hototo shook his head agreeably. "Yes, my son, the cyclops. He is but one of many monsters I have heard about. You must be very careful and cautious on your travels, and never fight unless it is absolutely necessary. Although I do not like you going so far, please travel prepared Marcellinus. I want you to remember that I will always love you."

Marcellinus looked pleased. "Thank you, Father; I love you, too. I am doing this so we can live a better life and I will be able to take care of you."

Hototo looked at Marcellinus a bit sadly. "Yes I know, and I am very proud to hear you say that. Just come back to me in one piece, okay, my son?"

Marcellinus looked at his father with a smile. "Of course. You trained me very well. It will take more than a cyclops to take me down. But I am curious as to what other monsters you have heard about."

Hototo looked even more worried. "I have heard tales of giant birds, giant spiders, dragons, and unholy spirits."

Marcellinus looked a little worried. "Oh, I see…then I shall do my best to avoid these beasts."

Hototo looked at him. "Yes, that would be wise. But just in case, you should take all my weapons; you may need them. Monsters are not your only problem, my son, for you must be on constant watch for the Roman legionnaires as well. They will kill you on sight."

Marcellinus looked very determined. "Of course, I will do my best, Father. I will make a safe path for Emperor Wu and then I shall return and we will both live in the biggest house our gold can buy." With that said, they both turned in for the night.

The next morning, Marcellinus packed everything he would need in his sack, from food to extra clothes. He sheathed his sword and placed it behind his back, along with his quiver of arrows. His bow he attached to his back as well. As for his knives, he harnessed them to his sides. Picking up everything, he ventured towards the door. "Father, I am leaving."

Hototo looked at Marcellinus and spoke. "Why are you traveling with no shirt and just pants, my son? Why do you not use the armor I have?"

Marcellinus looked a bit frustrated, as he knew this question would come. "You need the armor more than I, Father. You are sick. You can sell it to get more coins for your medicine. Since I will be gone for a long time, you need a way to get money."

Hototo sadly said, "My son, what about the dangers? Are you sure you will be fine?"

Marcellinus just chuckled. "Do not worry about me, Father. I will be completely fine. After all, I was trained by the best swordsman in all of China." Hototo and Marcellinus looked at each other with smiles as Marcellinus made his way out the door.

Hototo did not own any horses, so Marcellinus would have to make his way to and fro on foot—a long journey indeed. As Marcellinus made his way down the path, Hototo yelled out, "Marcellinus!" Marcellinus turned to look. "I love you, my son!"

Marcellinus, with a tear rolling down his cheek, said, "I love you, too, Father. When I return, we can live a rich and happy life—you, me and Princess Nangong. You will see, Father! I will make you proud!" And with that, Marcellinus began to run down the path, starting his impossible journey.

Hototo watched as his son ran out in the distance. "I know you will, son, I know you will. I have been proud of you since the day I found you."

# Chapter 3

Marcellinus ran until he reached the gate that bordered Chang'an. The guard immediately stepped forward. "Halt! Who goes there?"

Marcellinus paused. "I am Marcellinus. I am on a quest for Emperor Wu himself to create a path of trade from Chang'an to the city of Syria."

The guard nodded as if he knew Marcellinus. "Oh it's you. Yes, I've heard about you, and your foolish quest." And with a chuckle, the guard continued, "Very well. I shall grant you passage. Good luck; you're going to need it Xirong! Ha, ha, ha, ha!" And with that, the guard gave the signal to open the gate and Marcellinus ran through while the guards looked at him and laughed.

As Marcellinus ran, he began to feel a little nervous, for he had never been outside the walls of Chang'an. The nervousness quickly went away, though, as he saw beautiful hills covered with a rainbow assortment of flowers and many wild animals prancing around. He felt at peace as he made his way to Lanzhou.

It was soon nightfall, and Marcellinus decided to make camp. Never had he slept outside before, but that didn't stop him from trying. He laid out some blankets of fur and gathered some wood to build a fire. He pulled out some food from his sack and began to feast. After his dinner, Marcellinus looked at the sky. Never had he seen such a beautiful sight. The moon was shining bright, and the stars littered the sky with brilliant sparkles of white. As he stared into the sky, he seemed at peace with himself, and soon he lay his head down and fell asleep.

The next morning, Marcellinus quickly gathered his things and continued his journey. It would be another day and night before Marcellinus would reach Lanzhou.

Upon his arrival in Lanzhou, Marcellinus looked around in amazement. Never had he seen a village like this before. It didn't compare to the Imperial City, of course, but it was just as peaceful. All the houses were made of stone and looked just like his father Hototo's home. Children were running around, playing, and people were shopping or feasting. He did notice, however, that many people were staring at him in a strange way. *I guess that is to be expected, for they probably have not seen too many travelers.* Marcellinus only stopped for a moment to admire the scenery, and then he would be on his way.

Just as he neared the edge of the village, he heard an older woman cry for help. He turned to look and saw an elderly lady slowly limping towards town with her back arched. "Help! Help!" she screamed, "Pangrandawu has my son! Please help! He will surely be eaten!"

Hearing this, Marcellinus stopped and ran towards the old woman, who was already surrounded by many villagers. "He's probably dead already!" yelled one man. "There is nothing we can do. Pangrandawu is too strong! No one can defeat him!" yelled another man. "The boy knows better than to play near his cave!" yelled a woman.

Marcellinus approached the crowd and spoke. "I am Marcellinus, I am a skilled warrior. Please tell me of this Pangrandawu."

One male villager smirked at Marcellinus and spoke. "Who cares if you're skilled? No one can defeat Pangrandawu!"

Marcellinus angrily said "It does not matter! Just tell me about him and where he lives!"

The man got a little scared and backed off while saying, "All right, all right! If you want to die so badly then I'll tell you. Pangrandawu is a giant, about the size of two trees, and he feasts on the flesh of man. No one has ever returned from his cave."

Marcellinus looked at the old woman, "Woman, tell me, where does Pangrandawu live?"

The old woman pointed north past the hills. "He lives just over those hills, about half a day's travel, in a large cave."

Marcellinus grabbed the old woman by the shoulder. "Do not worry, woman; I will save your son."

After that, Marcellinus departed for the cave of Pangrandawu. All the villagers thought he was very foolish and would surely die, except the old lady, who began to pray for his safe return with her son. Marcellinus was very nervous indeed, for he had never fought a monster before, or for that matter, had never seen one either. Knowing he couldn't just leave that poor child to die, Marcellinus knew something had to be done.

After a while, he arrived at the cave of the Pangrandawu. Many human bones and skulls littered the ground near the beast's cave. It was exceedingly dark inside, and he could only see the green moss stretching over the mouth of the cave. Marcellinus then took some cloth from his sack and wrapped it around an arrow and started a fire with a stone and some wood. He lit the cloth on his arrow so as to make a torch. He ventured inside the cave and began to smell a horrid smell of rotting flesh as the torch scared a nearby group of bats out of the cave. Knowing the noise might have attracted the attention of Pangrandawu, Marcellinus quickly drew his sword.

He continued a little deeper into the cave and still heard and saw nothing. Was he too late? Had the boy been killed? Perhaps the monster wasn't inside at the moment? Just then, he heard a soft rumbling sound coming from the back of the cave. Marcellinus raised the torch higher to see if he could make it out, but the rumbling turned to a growl as a huge creature started dashing towards him. Marcellinus quickly turned to escape the darkness of the cave, for he knew he would not be able to fight the beast in the dark. He made it out of the cave with the rumbling of the ground closing in behind him, and he knew the beast was close. As he exited, he turned back and saw a giant club crashing down towards him, so he quickly dove to the left to avoid being squashed. As he rose to his feet, he saw the abomination known as Pangrandawu standing before him. It was truly a sight to behold as he stood in the entrance of the cave. The creature let out a mighty growl, like the sound of a titanic bear.

The monstrosity had but one eye, of a yellowish tint. Its ears were pointy like an elf's, and the skin was a musty green color adorned with many warts and blemishes. The feet were in the odd shape of an elephant's. Its mouth was rather large indeed, layered with two rows of razor sharp teeth. In its hands was a rather crude club used for a weapon, which was obviously made from the trunk of a tree, with some slight modifications. The club was layered with large wooden spikes that the creature seemed to have embedded into it. As the monster stood to howl at the sky, Marcellinus could see just how tall it really was, standing at least two tree lengths high. Spit and slime flew from the creature's mouth as the beast smashed the ground with its club once more, as if to intimidate Marcellinus. Then Marcellinus made a shocking discovery: the creature had the young boy strapped to its side, so Marcellinus knew he wasn't too late and he made it just in time.

First thing was first: Marcellinus had to free the boy. As the monster came stomping towards Marcellinus, Marcellinus dove to the right side, where the boy was, and with a swift swing of his sword, managed to cut the boy free. "Go! Run and hide!" Marcellinus told the boy. And the child did just that. Enraged at having lost the boy, Pangrandawu began charging towards Marcellinus. Marcellinus dove once more out of the reach of the mighty beast's club. Pangrandawu was strong and large, but its size made it difficult to move quickly, which Marcellinus used to his advantage. After dodging a few more attacks, Marcellinus went in for the kill. With a sharp slice to the creature's wrist he caused it to drop its mighty club as blood poured out from the wound. It then grabbed the wound to comfort it with the other hand, but then released it quickly. As the beast tried to recover his club, Marcellinus, seeing this as his chance, dashed in and sliced the beast three times in the stomach, but it still wasn't enough, because the beast tried to smash Marcellinus with its fist. Marcellinus dashed to the left quickly, the fist just missing him. *Its skin is tougher than stone*, Marcellinus thought. It seemed he would have to go for the throat. The beast recovered from his wounds and managed to get its club back. But in doing so, it left another opening for Marcellinus to attack. Using his knife, Marcellinus pierced the back of the beast and hopped on the back of the mighty titan, using the knife as leverage. Pangrandawu tried desperately to grab Marcellinus from its back and even tried shaking him off, but to no avail. Marcellinus was too quick. In a matter of seconds, Marcellinus had scaled the mighty beast and reached its neck. Marcellinus grabbed his sword and, with a mighty slash, cut the beast's neck. Screaming in agony, it grabbed its throat in pain while blood dripped down its chest. Then, without pause, Marcellinus raised his sword high in the air and plunged the sword deep into the creature's skull.

The beast screamed so loudly the entire country of China, it seemed, could hear it, if for only a moment. Then the eye of the creature rolled back in its head and, with a thunderous smash, it crashed down to the ground, dead. Marcellinus removed his sword from the mighty beast and cleaned off the blood on some nearby grass. He sheathed his sword once more and stared at the carcass of the beast. Marcellinus was a bit shaken up but very proud of his achievement. He had now gained some new confidence in himself. Taking down this beast took some skill and was no easy task. He then realized that he did indeed have what it took to complete his quest.

Marcellinus called out to the boy, "Boy! It is safe! The beast is dead!" At once the child ran towards Marcellinus with tears flowing down his face. Marcellinus got down on one knee and smiled. "Come, let us take you back to the village…back to your mother." With a smile, the boy nodded and held Marcellinus's hand as they made their way back to the village.

Upon their arrival, the townspeople all gathered quickly around the two with such excitement and glee. People were shouting things like "Unbelievable!" and "Amazing!" The one heard most was, "We must celebrate! Pangrandawu, the horrible cyclops, is dead!"

The old woman reunited with her child with tears in her eyes, and she looked at Marcellinus. "Thank you, great warrior, thank you. My son is all I have left."

Marcellinus looked at the woman with loving eyes. "Of course. It was an honor to have saved your son." He looked at the boy. "Now you need to promise me you will always take care of your mother, okay? She needs you to take care of her and protect her. No more running off."

The boy nodded and hugged Marcellinus and said, "Yeah, I'm going to grow up strong like you and kill any monsters that get in my way!" Marcellinus just laughed and rubbed the boy's head.

The elder and leader of the village came over to Marcellinus and spoke. "Thank you, kind stranger. That beast Pangrandawu has plagued my village for countless generations. Please, it would be an honor if I could have you for a celebratory feast tonight."

Marcellinus nodded. "I will accept your kind offer, thank you."

Later that evening, a mighty feast was held to celebrate the defeat of the titan Pangrandawu. Never before had Marcellinus seen such a sight. There was dancing by beautiful women, wonderful rhythmic music, and so much food that it could feed the imperial army easily. They feasted and drank throughout the night as Marcellinus told the story of how he defeated the beast time and time again.

At last, morning came and Marcellinus awoke knowing he had a quest to complete. Marcellinus made his way out of the house he had slept in and gathered his belongings. The village elder then approached him. "Are you sure you do not wish to stay, Marcellinus? We would more than welcome you here."

Marcellinus, with a disappointed look on his face, said, "No, I have a quest to complete. I must be on my way."

The village elder seemed disappointed. "Then please take whatever supplies you need, and I wish you the best of luck my friend." With a smile, Marcellinus thanked him and made his way to the merchant to stock up on everything he possibly could, and he started on his way out of the village. As he ran off towards the distance, he turned to see the whole village standing there waving at him and cheering. He waved back and smiled. He then turned around and continued his long journey to Syria.

# Chapter 4

Marcellinus traveled for ten more days and nights before he entered the next village. It was a small village compared to Lanzhou. As he entered the village, Marcellinus saw many people lying on the ground with their hands upon their stomachs, obviously starving to death. It was truly a sight to behold, for these people looked like walking skeletons.

Marcellinus found the nearest healthy person he could and began to speak. "Excuse me, what village is this?"

The person looked at Marcellinus with a distraught face, and with a melancholic voice began to speak. "This is Jiayuguan."

Marcellinus then looked around at the starving people and asked the man, "What has happened here?"

The man, still distraught, told him a most shocking tale. "We are starving to death. For many months now, the great king of birds, Fenghuang, has been ravaging our crops. He has eaten every last bit of our food. All attempts to attack him have failed. It only makes him madder and he begins to attack the village and our people." Marcellinus got very teary-eyed as he saw the dying bodies of children on the ground. How could this creature do this to this poor village? Marcellinus knew the bird must pay.

Placing a hand on the shoulder of the man, Marcellinus spoke. "Have no fear, my friend, for I am Marcellinus. I have been trained by Hototo Takeshi, the greatest swordsman in all of China. Show me these crops, and I will kill this beast, Fenghuang."

The man seemed a bit happy that this stranger would help the village recover from this tragedy as he spoke. "Oh really? Thank you so much! The fields are just over that way, to the east of here. It is about a quarter of a day's journey." With that said, Marcellinus quickly made his way over to the fields. As he was running, the man told him, "Please save the crops! These are our last batch. If they go, we all will die very soon! Good luck!"

It didn't take long for Marcellinus to reach the crop fields. He saw no beast in sight, so he decided to hide and wait in some nearby bushes for the mighty bird's arrival. It had now been

Matthew Rodriguez

quite a while since Marcellinus had chosen to hide. Just as he was about to give up for the day, he heard a terrible screech coming from the sky. He looked up to see a massive bird fly down and land on the ground below. The gargantuan bird then cautiously twitched its head back and forth to make sure the coast was clear, and once it was sure it was safe, it bent down and began feasting on the crop.

As Marcellinus readied his bow and arrows, he saw that it was truly a beautiful bird. The massive bird stood about one tree length high. It had the head and comb of a pheasant, while the tail was very similar to a peacock's. Brilliant blue, green, and white feathers adorned its entire body. The spots on the tail shone with rainbow-like brilliance. Its head was actually quite small compared to the rest of the body, which was equipped with two small, green, antennae-like feathers on top. The blue head ended with a very small beak as well, and it also had the tiniest eyes Marcellinus had seen on a beast.

Marcellinus saw an opportunity to attack as it feasted. He quietly brought his bow and arrow around to the front, being careful to not make any rustling noises within the bushes. Marcellinus took an arrow and quickly tied a long piece of rope to the front end of it. He tied the other end to a very large boulder that was near the bushes. He made sure Fenghuang was facing the other direction before he crawled towards the boulder and fastened it around while hiding behind the stone. Then, like lightning, Marcellinus jumped up and shot the arrow in between the yellow chicken-like legs of the beast. Startled, Fenghuang began to move his other leg to run and fly away. But this was very foolish, as when the beast did this, it caused the rope to circle and intertwine its legs, just as Marcellinus wanted. With a crash, the bird smacked the ground. Marcellinus then charged at the now helpless beast. Seeing the initial threat, Fenghuang began using his sharp beak and in no time at all had cut through the rope like a knife through paper. Marcellinus saw the bird taking off, and he thought he had lost his chance. But with his last bit of speed, Marcellinus lunged at the bird and stabbed the bird in the back end with one of his knives. Marcellinus was now flying high in the air, holding on to the knife with all his might. The wind current was incredible. Marcellinus could hardly move for the force would surely blow him off. Fenghuang was screeching quite loudly now and, trying to dispatch his stowaway, began dive-bombing at incredible speeds. But Marcellinus was still holding on. Frustrated, Fenghuang headed for some nearby trees and attempted to ram Marcellinus into them, in hopes he would fall off his back. Marcellinus survived ram after ram from the oncoming trees, but the majority of them he managed to swing away from. Fenghuang saw this was not working either so he began to flap his wings to fly higher. Marcellinus realized, as Fenghuang flapped, that the wind current wasn't as strong; perhaps this was his chance. Marcellinus pulled himself up by grabbing Fenghuang's feathers and slowly climbed up the bird's back. Marcellinus unsheathed his sword and aimed for the left wing of the beast. Fenghuang, sensing danger, then did a complete barrel roll in the sky. Marcellinus lost his balance but quickly grabbed a massive chunk of the beast's feathers. Surviving barrel roll after barrel roll, Marcellinus finally had enough and slashed the beast in the side with his blade. The bird, now in pain, returned to a straight flight path again. Marcellinus stood up once more and raised his sword high in the air. As blood oozed out of the previous cut, he slashed his sword down and began to cut the left wing off. After two successful slashes, the wing came completely off. Blood was now raining from the sky, as the gargantuan bird plummeted towards earth once more. Marcellinus knew the bird would surely die, as would he, once they hit ground. So as the bird spiraled down towards the ground, Marcellinus readied to jump, and just as Fenghuang hit the ground, Marcellinus leaped off the body to the left and rolled many times. Fenghuang hit the ground hard and broke his neck in several places. Marcellinus could hear the sound of cracking bones as he continued to roll. After the dust settled, Marcellinus rose from the ground, a little beaten up but otherwise fine. He then approached the crater surrounding Fenghuang's broken body and took his sword and cut the head off. Marcellinus picked it up and made his way back to Jiayuguan.

Upon his arrival, he was greeted by the same man. "So how did you fare, traveler?"

With a smirk, Marcellinus showed him the decapitated head of Fenghuang. "This foul beast shall trouble you no more!"

The man was overjoyed and began running up and down the streets, screaming, "Fenghuang is dead! Our crops are safe once more! Praise be to the brave traveler!" After many thank yous and praises, Marcellinus decided to continue on his journey. The people of Jiayuguan promised never to forget Marcellinus and decided to build a monument for him one day, as the king of birds' slayer. Marcellinus waved at his newfound friends and ran out of the village towards his next stop. As for Fenghuang's head, the villagers decided to enshrine it in a makeshift altar. They placed the mummified head in a small ornate box, as a reminder of all the terrible things it did and to remind them of Marcellinus, their greatest hero. To this day, no one knows what happened to the head of Fenghuang; perhaps it was buried and lost over time.

# Chapter 5

Another seven days and nights went by before Marcellinus reached the next village. As he entered, he saw that it was much larger than the previous two villages, and many armor - clad men and women stood around, talking, laughing, feasting, and drinking. Marcellinus felt very comfortable here. Just as he was walking past some stone houses, he noticed a rather large building serving alcohol and fresh food. Then a middle-aged man came barging out the doors, obviously drunk, and stumbled onto Marcellinus's shoulder. Marcellinus kind of frowned as he shrugged the man off. The man spoke with very slurred words as he slapped Marcellinus on the back. "How are you, my boy? Are you also here for the treasure?"

Marcellinus looked at him, puzzled. "Treasure? What matter do you speak of?"

The armor-clad man rolled his eyes and said, "The treasure, son! The treasure! Don't tell me you haven't heard of it! Everyone from here to the city of Altay knows about it!" The man continued his drunken rambling. "They say if you can survive the labyrinth and best the beast within, the Ifrit, then the treasure of unsurpassable wonders awaits you!" As tempting as this sounded, Marcellinus knew he had a quest to finish. So he bumped aside the man and started to make his way out of town. The man started rambling some more. "Oh no you don't! I'll get that treasure first or my name isn't…" Just then, the man passed out from being so drunk. Marcellinus shook his head and continued.

He happened to pass by a woman and man talking to each other and heard their conversation very briefly. The man spoke first. "Yeah, she headed over to the labyrinth with hardly any protection. I warned her not to go but she refused to listen."

The woman then continued the conversation. "She has always been like that. She thinks she can get the treasure so she can give it to her family. But she doesn't realize that no one has come out of there alive." Hearing this, Marcellinus became interested, for there was another on a quest similar to his. A treasure to take care of her family—he knew that story all too well. If she was in trouble, perhaps he could help her get the treasure, he thought.

"Excuse me," Marcellinus interrupted. "This woman you speak of, who is she?"

The man and woman both looked at Marcellinus, puzzled. "Why do you want to know?" the man asked.

Marcellinus paused for but a moment and thought up a lie quickly. "Oh, my apologies. I am Marcellinus. I am a wandering traveler interested in the treasure."

The woman looked at Marcellinus and spoke. "Oh really? Then you better hurry before Aloisia runs off with it." Then the man and woman began to laugh.

"I see," said Marcellinus. He quickly asked, "Where is this treasure?"

The woman smiled and looked at him. "Ah, trying to beat her to the treasure, I see. It's great to see a *real* warrior around here. Most of these guys are all talk and would never really try to get the treasure. If you go west from here, about half a day's travel, you will come upon a large cave. Inside, you will find a labyrinth and your treasure."

Marcellinus thanked the woman, but before he left, he asked one more question. "Could you please tell me about this Ifrit I've been hearing about?"

The man decided to answer this one. "Sure. Ifrit is the monster who guards the treasure inside the cave. As if the tricks and traps of the labyrinth weren't bad enough, this creature makes it worse. As for what it looks like, I'm not really sure. No one who has seen it has lived to talk about it. But I *have* heard stories, but they could be lies. They say it is as large as a man, and has horns atop its head, and is supposedly very quick."

Marcellinus looked worried. *A demon?* he thought. Marcellinus then thanked the two as they wished him luck.

He ran towards the cave of the Ifrit. After not long at all, he reached a monstrous cave. A sign outside read, "Cave of Ifrit. Adventurers beware!" Taking the words to heart, Marcellinus slowly made his way inside. As he entered, he noticed that this cave was very large indeed. The walls were adorned with many torches that were set aflame. *Plenty of light*, Marcellinus thought. Marcellinus looked at the walls and noticed they were made of a strange orange brick of some kind—something he had never seen before. He walked down the path that seemed to stretch for miles. Suddenly, he came to a three-way split. *Which way?* he thought. Not really knowing which way to go, Marcellinus headed towards the right. As he stepped, he triggered a switch on the floor. Suddenly, a large battering ram, adorned with spikes, swung full speed from the ceiling. With a grunt, Marcellinus quickly dropped to the floor. The battering ram had barely missed him. As it stopped swinging, Marcellinus rose to his feet once more and wiped the sweat from his brow. *Too close*, he thought. Marcellinus realized just how dangerous this place really was, so he unsheathed his sword to prepare for what was next to come. He continued down the right path for a while, only to find it led to a dead end. Frustrated, Marcellinus made his way back to the first split. Upon arriving back, he had two more choices: straight or left. He decided to head straight this time. He slowly stepped forward, being careful not to trigger any more switches. As he neared the end, he noticed a large piece of ground elevated above the rest. There was clearly no way around it, and it was too large to jump over. So he had no choice but to step on it. As he did, he readied his sword because he heard the sound of grinding stone. Like magic, the walls in front of him opened up, creating a pathway. He started to walk forward, only to notice small holes on the wall, which after a few seconds began spitting small darts. Marcellinus didn't want to traverse this trap, but as he turned around, he noticed the way he came from had now closed, trapping him here. The switch was also no longer usable. Having no choice, Marcellinus had to dodge the oncoming darts. As the first one shot, and before another shot, he jumped in front of the hole. While rolling under the next hole, he rose to his feet and quickly leaped over the next trap. He then ran swiftly past the next one, efficiently eluding the oncoming dart. He reached the final set, which was shooting three darts at a time, one at head level, the other in the middle, and the last at the feet. Standing in a cramped zone safe from the previous darts, he readied his sword. With a mighty leap, Marcellinus leaped over the bottom two darts and placed his sword along his body on his left side, making a crude long and thin shield, so when he jumped, the dart just bounced right off. He got to the next split, this time with two ways to go. Irritated, he took the left path. As he turned the corner, he noticed a rope hanging from the ceiling in the middle of the floor. Puzzled, he cautiously made his way forward, and as he stepped in the middle, he heard a snapping sound as the floor gave way beneath him, revealing a deadly spike trap below. Reacting immediately, Marcellinus grabbed the rope, hoping it wasn't a trap as well. Marcellinus was now hanging safely over the hole. He looked down to notice the blood-stained spikes below with an assortment of bones decorating them. He then began to swing back and forth and leaped to the other side. "This place is a nightmare," he said to himself. He then began to worry about the female warrior's safety. He hoped she was fine.

After many more twists and turns and several dead ends, Marcellinus was beginning to become tired. *How much farther does this go?* he thought. He slowly made his way around each turn. The spike trap was the last trap that was seen for a while. He came across a long hallway with eight paths leading to the left, and none to the right. *Great,* he thought. As Marcellinus neared them, flames began spewing forth from the many holes along the left and right walls. Timing each one very carefully, he leaped, jumped, and ran past them all. He eventually got to a gap in the flames at about the fifth path on the left. Seeing this as a sign, he ventured forth down this path. He walked down it, wondering where the Ifrit could be and if the female warrior was okay. As he neared the end, he could hear a faint whimpering in the distance. Not knowing what it could be, he readied his sword. He then heard a female voice say, "Hello? Who's there? Is someone there? Please! Help me!" Marcellinus, hearing this, quickly rushed towards the voice. As he neared it, he noticed it was coming from the mouth of a beautiful female warrior. So beautiful in fact that Marcellinus shortly paused while walking towards her. As he got closer, he noticed her predicament: she was trapped in a room surrounded by bars. The woman was being held prisoner. Marcellinus approached the barbaric cell and, in the light of the flame, he managed to get a good look at her. She was quite beautiful indeed. The woman had hair as black as the night sky. It was cut short but still had a small ponytail in the back. She stood at about five feet seven inches. The woman was wearing impressive silver armor that covered her shoulders, her entire legs, her arms, her hips, and her chest. The armor on her chest didn't cover it all the way, however, for only her breasts and ribs were covered. She had a gap in the middle of her chest armor, revealing her stomach and belly button as well as her cleavage. The woman also seemed to be wearing some sort of iron boots on her feet. She had a red cloth-like loincloth on, which matched her red under-armor. The woman also carried with her a massive spear that she must use as her weapon. The weapon was quite impressive. It had an extended handle made of wood with a thirty-five-inch blade attached to the end. Her eyes were a beautiful hazel color, and her skin was silky smooth with a beige tan to it.

No matter her beauty, Marcellinus knew he must find a way to help her, and he must stay loyal to Princess Nangong. He approached the bars and tried to squeeze them together in hopes they'd break, but to no avail. He then spoke. "It's no use. I cannot break these bars." The female warrior got a little restless as she began to cry. Marcellinus then tried to calm her down as he tried to figure a way out. "Woman, calm down. I shall figure a way out for you." Just then, Marcellinus heard a terrible sound from the other end of the hallway. It sounded like a grunting bull or possibly a cow. He turned to look, with his sword at the ready, and then he saw it. A monstrous beast walked around the corner and turned to face him. Marcellinus got a good look at it. *What kind of abomination is this?* he thought.

"It's the Ifrit!" the woman cried. The beast stood at the end of the hall towering before Marcellinus. It clearly was about seven feet tall. The creature was half man and half bull. A disgusting sight to behold. It's muscles were five times larger than the rest of its body. The feet were hoofed like a bull's, with weird spike-like appendages protruding from its shins. The beast wore a crude loincloth made from the fur of animals. Although the beast could not speak, it was clear that the monstrosity was more intelligent than the last two, for the creature was wearing some crude but fashionable battle gear. It had arm wraps on, as well as a strap going across its human-like chest to its back, with the picture of a human skull on it. Unlike a real bull, the beast wasn't hairy at all. Upon its shoulder sat a massive skull from some sort of creature, which the creature seemed to be using as a makeshift shoulder pad. In its hands it held a massive hammer, with the hammer end as large as Marcellinus's whole body. At the opposite end of the hammer, on the handle end, it was adorned with a spike, obviously used for throwing, like a spear. It was large but easily carried by the human-like hands of the buff beast. Although the beast did not have a tail, its face was the complete embodiment of a bull. It had massive horns protruding from its skull and beady red eyes. The monster sported a short beard, piercings in both ears, and a rather large nose ring, as well.

Marcellinus then hatched a plan. Maybe he could get Ifrit to charge at him and he would smash through the wall, freeing the woman. With that thought, Marcellinus told the woman to move to the side, for he had a plan. He looked back at Ifrit, who was slowly making its way towards Marcellinus, howling and snorting like a bull. Without a second thought, Marcellinus readied his bow and arrow and shot an arrow at the beast. The beast was too smart for that and quickly dodged the arrow, but as Ifrit moved to the left side to dodge the arrow, Marcellinus pulled out a knife and threw it at the creature. Although Ifrit missed the arrow, it could not dodge the knife. It plunged deep in its side. Enraged, the mighty beast pulled the knife out and blood poured out. Then, with a mighty roar, Ifrit made ready to charge, just like a real bull. Ifrit came full speed at Marcellinus, who jumped to the side at the last moment, sending the beast smashing through the stone wall and iron bars, freeing the woman. She and Marcellinus quickly united with each other. The woman then asked, "Is it dead?"

Marcellinus paused and took a brief look inside and heard and saw nothing but dust. He then said, "I don't know, but we must leave now, quickly!" Marcellinus and the woman made their way to the end of the hall and noticed the flame traps were off. Puzzled, they began to run in the direction Marcellinus came in from. They both thought to themselves that perhaps Ifrit turned off the traps before he attacked. They only got lost once or twice and finally saw the entrance to the cave. As they were running to exit the cave, the woman stopped and yelled, "Wait! I cannot leave without the treasure!"

Marcellinus, thinking that to be foolish, yelled back, "Woman, do you want to die? It is too dangerous. Ifrit or the traps will surely kill you. They could be turned on again!"

The woman said with anger, "I don't care! I need the treasure to help my family!"

As she ran towards the labyrinth once again, the ground began to shake as they heard loud grunting. Marcellinus then yelled, "The beast lives! We must go now!" They began to hear smash after smash as they saw bits and pieces of rock and rubble fly through the air. The beast then smashed its way through the last wall to the entrance of the cave, confronting the two warriors. The beast continued its charge, using the mighty hammer to smack the female warrior across the room, knocking her unconscious. Marcellinus then readied his sword. As Ifrit swung its mighty hammer, Marcellinus ducked and sliced Ifrit's beefy leg. Hardly feeling a thing, Ifrit swung the hammer again, this time hitting Marcellinus in his side. Marcellinus flew across the room onto the ground. Ifrit did not stop there, though, for the beast tried to smash Marcellinus once more with the hammer as he lay there helpless. Marcellinus quickly rolled left, leaving a hole in the ground where the hammer smashed instead. Then the beast tried once more, and Marcellinus then rolled back to the right. As Ifrit tried once more, Marcellinus drew his blade and gave the beast a quick slice in the same leg again, this time widening the cut. Ifrit was now in severe pain and it got down on one knee. Marcellinus stood up and only had time to swing his sword once, but the beast recovered and blocked Marcellinus's swing with its hammer. Sword and wood clashed, and now a test of strength ensued. Marcellinus knew the beast was much stronger then he was, so he had to act quickly. He gave it quick kick to the gut, and the beast had the wind knocked out of it. Then Marcellinus cut through the hammer, breaking off the tip. Ifrit quickly recovered and gave Marcellinus a hard punch to the face. Marcellinus once again flew to the ground. Ifrit picked up its broken hammer and made its way to Marcellinus slowly. Marcellinus was now badly beaten and suffered a mild concussion. Ifrit raised the broken hammer in the air, with the handle end with the spike facing down towards Marcellinus. Marcellinus quickly grabbed his sword to try and block the incoming attack, but just as the beast was lunging down, a massive blade cut through its body from back to front. Screaming in agony, the beast dropped his weapon and began to try and pull the weapon out from its back.

As Ifrit turned, Marcellinus saw his savior, the female warrior. "Now we're even," she said. Marcellinus rose to his feet and, with a firm grip on his sword, approached the twisting and turning Ifrit. With five mighty slashes on the stomach, the beast crumpled to the ground. Dealing a final blow, Marcellinus beheaded Ifrit. Blood began pouring out of the neck wound with a barely visible spine showing. Marcellinus, exhausted, dropped to the ground as he grabbed his side in pain. The female warrior approached Marcellinus, "Are you okay? You look pretty bad."

Marcellinus arose and spoke. "I'll be fine. What about you? Are you okay?"

She wiped some dried blood from her head and answered, "I'm all right. Just a little cut on my head is all."

They both looked inside the cave. With the walls smashed, it would be very easy to recover the treasure now. They both then made their way inside. All the traps still seemed to be turned off. After a few more twists and turns, they finally came to a stone door. They pushed against it and, with both their strength, pushed it aside, revealing a small room with mountains upon mountains of gold everywhere. It was truly a beautiful sight. Marcellinus and the female warrior took only what they could carry and made their way out of the cave once more. The female warrior then spoke to Marcellinus. "I need to get back home. I must tell my brothers about the treasure so they can come back and get some more."

Marcellinus looked at the warrior. "Very well. Then go. I hope you and your family live a very good life."

The female warrior then slightly blushed and said to Marcellinus, "W-would you like to accompany me? I'm sure my mother has some herbs and bandages to help you heal." Marcellinus looked at her a bit weary-eyed. "Please? I want to help you," she said.

Marcellinus smiled at her. "All right, then. I shall accompany you home." Then the two slowly made their way back to the village.

# Chapter 6

As the two walked, they held many conversations so as to get to know each other better. Marcellinus was the first to speak. "So do you live within the village as well?"

The female warrior then looked at him and began talking. "No, not really. I live with my mother and two brothers in a small cottage on the outskirts of town."

Marcellinus nodded, and continued, "Oh I see. So what is your name? I am Marcellinus."

The woman smiled and said, "My name is Aloisia."

"Aloisia, what a beautiful name," Marcellinus said with a smile. Aloisia just blushed.

After a short pause, she started talking once more, "So, Marcellinus, what brings you out here to Hami?"

Marcellinus got quite serious once again as he began to tell Aloisia the story of how he was on a quest for Emperor Wu to make a trading route, which he was doing this to help his father, Hototo, live a better life. And then he said, "That is why, when I heard the couple talk about a woman going to the cave to get treasure to help her family, I knew I had to help you. For I know what it's like to not have money to take care of your loved ones."

Aloisia blushed even more than before, "Oh, I see. Well thank you, Marcellinus. Without your help, I would have surely been killed."

Marcellinus then asked her, "Aloisia, how did you get trapped in that prison within the labyrinth?"

She seemed a little embarrassed. "Well I made it through the traps, and once I reached the end, I confronted Ifrit. He easily knocked me unconscious and threw me in that cell."

Marcellinus felt bad, for maybe that question was a bit inappropriate. "Oh, well don't feel too bad, for if not for you, Ifrit surely would have killed me as well."

This made Aloisia feel a little better, "Yeah, you're right. I really saved your life back there, huh?" They both laughed.

Marcellinus began asking another question. "So how did your family end up in such need for money?"

Aloisia was a bit sad upon answering. "Well, it was when I was little. One day, a group of soldiers from Rome came and ransacked our village. They burned many houses, and my father tried to fight back but they killed him. As punishment, they took all our coins and burned down our house in the village. My brothers were also badly beaten." Marcellinus was very saddened to hear that this happened. She continued, "After that, I made a vow to one day avenge my father's death. I would never allow those soldiers to kill any more innocent people. So I decided to start training to fight on my own."

Marcellinus was pretty shocked to hear that and said, "Wow, you trained yourself to use that spear? Very impressive."

She smiled and said, "Thank you. It wasn't easy. It took me many years to perfect the technique, but once I heard about this treasure, I knew I just had to go and get it, no matter the cost. My family means everything to me, and I would do anything to help them." Marcellinus began to feel very proud and honored to be in her presence. She then turned to Marcellinus as she stopped walking and said, "You know, most people would frown on the fact that I'm a warrior. Many people believe that only men can become warriors and that women should stay home."

Marcellinus then looked back with a smile and said, "This is true, but I was raised by my father to respect all people, especially women, for they give the greatest gift of all, the gift of life."

Aloisia blushed once more. "Th-thank you. You don't act like a typical warrior, Marcellinus."

Marcellinus looked a little puzzled as he said, "I don't? Why not?"

She then smiled and said, "Well, you're too nice. Most warriors around here don't care about anyone but themselves, but you are different. You go out of your way to help those in need. This is a rare quality indeed."

Marcellinus looked a bit worried as he said, "Oh, is that a bad thing?"

Aloisia giggled as she said, "No, of course not. You are a great man." She blushed as she said, "Also, I think it's kind of cute."

Marcellinus blushed a bit as well as he said, "Oh…okay."

They walked a little more until they finally reached the cottage in which Aloisia lived. "We're here!" she said as she ran towards the door. "Mother! Brothers! I have returned with some treasure!" As Aloisia said this, her mother and brothers exited the cottage. Her brothers were both very tall men, standing at about six feet tall. They looked like twins. The only difference was one had a bald head and the other didn't. They both were pretty muscular as well. Aloisia's mother was also quite beautiful for her age. She looked just like Aloisia, just with gray hair.

One of the brothers spoke. "I can't believe you found the treasure. How did you do it?"

Aloisia then laughed as she punched him in the arm. "It's a secret!" The other brother turned to see Marcellinus out in the distance. He gave Marcellinus an evil stare.

Aloisia's mother began to speak. "Aloisia! I'm so glad you're safe! I was so worried about you!" She hugged her daughter with tears flowing from her eyes.

The brother spoke at Marcellinus, while still giving him evil eyes. "Who are you?"

Before Marcellinus could speak, Aloisia answered that question, "This is Marcellinus. He's my friend. He saved me from Ifrit, so be nice to him, brother." The brother just shrugged his shoulders and returned inside.

Aloisia told the other brother to retrieve the rest of the treasure soon, before the villagers find out that Ifrit is dead and make off with the rest of the gold. He promised to go with the other brother in the morning.

Aloisia looked at Marcellinus, who was still in pain, as she spoke to her mother. "Mother, can you please help Marcellinus? I'm sure we have some bandages and herbs for him, right?"

Her mother just smiled a little bit as she said, "Yes, I will try and help him as much as I can. Please come inside, Marcellinus."

Marcellinus then approached the cottage as he said, "Thank you very much. I truly appreciate it." The mother smiled as they all went inside.

Aloisia's mother had Marcellinus lay down on an old bed made of stone, with hay and cotton on top as a makeshift pillow and some fur blankets. Aloisia told Marcellinus that this was her bed. The mother came inside the room with many bandages and herbs. She ground up the herbs to make a patch of sorts to heal his wounds. After applying the patches to his wounds, Aloisia's mother wrapped him with the bandages. She spoke to him. "You should get some rest; you will heal faster."

Marcellinus didn't think he had time to rest, but the bed was very comfortable and he was completely exhausted. Perhaps a little nap wouldn't hurt. He smiled as he said, "Thank you for your generosity." Before he fell asleep, he told the mother, "I see where Aloisia gets her beauty from," as he smiled and then fell fast asleep.

The mother blushed and giggled and then looked at Aloisia and said, "Come, Aloisia, he needs his rest." Then they both left the room.

Marcellinus had a terrible nightmare. He dreamt of his father dying and crying out for Marcellinus to save him. As he lay tossing and turning, Aloisia walked by the room and stopped to watch him sleep and check on him. Just then, her mother walked down the hall towards her, startling Aloisia. Her mother said, "You like him, don't you?"

Shocked and blushing a bit, Aloisia said, "No, of course not! I was just checking on him is all."

Her mother rolled her eyes and said, "Oh come now, Aloisia. I'm your mother. I can tell when you are lying." The mother then looked at Marcellinus as Aloisia said not a word. The mother spoke. "He is fighting his fever from the wounds. When he wakes, he should be fine. Do not worry." The mother then patted Aloisia on the shoulder and walked away as Aloisia continued to watch him sleep.

Soon it was morning. Marcellinus leaped up from the bed, drenched in sweat. He then looked outside and realized it was morning. Panicked over losing so much time, he quickly began to gather his things to depart. As he was doing so, Aloisia came into the room. "Oh, Marcellinus! You are awake!" He didn't speak a word as he continued packing. Aloisia looked a bit sad as she said, "Leaving already?"

Marcellinus, with his stuff all packed, walked towards Aloisia and spoke. "Yes, I have a journey to finish. Thank you very much for your hospitality. Please take care of your family."

Aloisia was a bit saddened to hear this and, in a panic, she blurted out, "No, wait! At least eat before you go!" Marcellinus stopped as Aloisia continued, "Please, my mother has already prepared a meal for you. It would mean a lot to her if you stayed to eat it."

Marcellinus was a little uncomfortable, but he did not want to hurt her mother's feelings, for she had taken good care of him. He spoke. "All right. I will stay to eat, but I must leave afterwards."

Aloisia was a bit relieved as she spoke. "Thank you. Come with me. I hope you like it; it is wild boar."

Marcellinus made his way into the kitchen and was greeted by the mother. "Oh, you're awake! How are your wounds?"

Marcellinus smiled as he said, "Much better now; thank you very much for your help."

The mother said, "No problem. Without you, my daughter could be dead, after all." She continued, "Please sit down and have some food."

Marcellinus, Aloisia, and her mother all began to feast. Marcellinus told her mother why he was there and what he was trying to accomplish. Hearing this, the mother realized the danger of his quest.

The brothers then returned home with even more treasure. One was talking as he entered the cottage. "We got as much as we could, but the village is catching wind of Ifrit's demise." And then one of the brothers saw Marcellinus sitting down, eating. The brother then screamed, "What is this foreign trash still doing here? Leave! You are not welcome here." Aloisia and her mother were stunned at the brother's words.

Marcellinus then grabbed his things as he said, "I should go. Thank you again for your hospitality; I shall not forget it." He then made his way out the door while giving the brother an evil look. The brother got a bit nervous. Aloisia stood up and ran after Marcellinus. Stopping by her brother, she slapped him hard in the face. Her brother was shocked at what happened.

The mother then screamed, "How dare you talk to our guest like that! You have brought dishonor here!" The brother got sad and apologized, not meaning to bring dishonor to the home. The mother then began to follow Aloisia out the door.

Marcellinus was walking towards the woods back to Hami, when he heard Aloisia shout, "Marcellinus, please wait! My brother is a fool. He knows not what he says!"

Marcellinus turned around with a smile and said, "It is all right, Aloisia. I must continue my quest, anyway. Thank you for the lovely meal."

Aloisia's mother had now stepped outside and saw her daughter walking quickly towards the side of the cottage. Aloisia then turned towards Marcellinus once again and spoke. "Marcellinus, wait!" He stopped once again and turned around. Aloisia then picked up her spear and ran towards Marcellinus. "Please, let me go with you." Marcellinus and Aloisia's mother were both completely shocked.

Marcellinus then spoke. "But…what about your family?"

Aloisia smiled and said, "Do not worry. They have plenty of gold now. They will be fine."

Marcellinus, still a little shocked, continued, "And your mother? You should stay to protect her."

Aloisia, with a smirk, said, "Have you forgotten? I have two brothers." Marcellinus was at a loss for words, for he didn't really know what to say. Aloisia saw this and got very sad. She then spoke. "Fine. If you do not want me to go then I shall stay…perhaps you are not as I thought."

Marcellinus quickly said, "Wait! It is not that I don't want you to go; it is that it will be very dangerous. I do not want to see you get hurt is all."

Aloisia was a bit saddened and relieved at the same time as she said, "Do not worry, I can fend for myself. I will not get in your way. And I *want* to go with you. You saved my life like I saved yours. You were very nice to me and my mother. I want to make it up to you by helping you complete your quest. If you really respected women like you told me you do, then you would respect my decision to go with you."

Marcellinus was a bit saddened as he felt bad for not respecting her decision. He then looked up at her with a smile and said, "You're right, Aloisia. I'm sorry. If you still want to come with me, I would be honored to travel with you."

She then smiled and said, "It's okay! Please give me some time to get prepared, okay? It won't take long." With that, she went back inside.

Her mother then approached Marcellinus and said, "Please watch out for her, Marcellinus. She is a good warrior, but she means everything to me. Although I can't stop her from going with you, I can at least express my feelings to you."

He then said, "Do not worry. I shall protect her with my life.

" The mother then smiled at him and said, "I know you will. You know, she cares a lot for you." Marcellinus blushed without saying a word.

"I'm ready! Let's go!" they heard a voice scream from behind them. Aloisia had come out and was wearing her battle gear once again, with a sack around her back full of food and extra clothes. She also had her spear sheathed behind her. The mother walked over to her to say good-bye.

After a kiss and a hug, the mother spoke. "Please be careful, Aloisia. Do not make any foolish decisions."

Aloisia looked at her mother and said, "Do not worry, Mother. I won't. Besides, I have Marcellinus to protect me."

The mother then looked at her daughter once more and spoke. "Marcellinus is a good man. I haven't met such a good man since your father. Don't let him go, Aloisia."

She then looked at her mother and quietly said, "I won't." And with that, the two warriors started to make their way back to the village, as Aloisia's mother stood waving at them and wishing them luck.

As they neared the village, they saw many battles breaking out, with the warriors killing each other for the gold they recovered from the cave. Marcellinus then said, "It seems they have found out that Ifrit is dead."

Aloisia then spoke. "Yes, we eliminated Ifrit as the problem just to create a whole new one." They both looked on from a distance. Then Aloisia said, "Perhaps we should make our way around the village instead." Marcellinus nodded and they both did just that. They were now running towards the next destination of their journey.

# Chapter 7

As they exited Hami, it was getting close to nightfall. Marcellinus and Aloisia stopped to make camp. It would be a little awkward for Marcellinus since he never slept around a woman before. Marcellinus got the fire started as Aloisia set up the beds. After their tasks were complete and dinner was eaten, Marcellinus sat down by his bed and stared at the beautiful sky. Aloisia saw this and walked over to Marcellinus. She then spoke. "Marcellinus? What are you looking at?"

Marcellinus looked at her and said, "I am looking at the stars. They are the most beautiful thing in the world. After a hard day's travel, I like to stare at them, for it puts me at peace."

Aloisia just smiled at him and began to look up as well. She then spoke. "Yes, they are quite beautiful. My father used to take me outside at night when I was little. He would tell me all the names of the stars."

Marcellinus seemed a bit shocked. "The stars have names? Wow, I had no idea. I wish I knew their names."

Aloisia just laughed and said, "You didn't know the stars had names? Your father never taught you?"

A little embarrassed Marcellinus said, "No, my father was a scholar, not an astronomer. He studied books instead of stars."

Aloisia seemed nervous and hoped she hadn't offended him. She then said, "Oh, I'm sorry, I had no idea." She then grabbed onto Marcellinus's hand and continued, "If you want, I can teach you the names."

Marcellinus blushed as he nervously let Aloisia hold his hand, "Yes, please. If it is not too much trouble." Then they both stared at the brilliant display of stars as the night went on.

In a few days' time, they would reach the next village. "The village of Urumqi," Aloisia said with a sigh of relief. Urumqi was a huge village. There were tons of shops and houses as far as the eye could see. People were running from shop to shop, buying everything they could see.

Marcellinus thought this to be strange and said, "This place is very busy. Something must be going on." The pair then made their way to the center of the village, where many people were gathered.

As they approached, they heard the voice of a man shouting, "We must do something! Asmodeus has plagued our forest long enough! Because of that foul beast, we can't even leave the boundaries of the city!" They both looked to see where the voice was coming from, and they saw a middle-aged man standing upon the stone steps of the nearby large building.

Marcellinus then spoke to Aloisia. "The man spoke of a beast named Asmodeus. Should we listen?"

Aloisia gave Marcellinus a smirk,. "Well of course we should. If we help, we could be rewarded."

Marcellinus didn't really care for a reward; he just wanted to help those in need. He then made his way to the front, while Aloisia hastily followed behind. The man was still screaming all sorts of things as the pair neared the front. Marcellinus then stepped up to where the man was, with Aloisia close behind, and spoke. "I am Marcellinus! I am a traveling warrior. What is this Asmodeus of which you speak?"

The man was a bit frustrated from being interrupted and said, "Who cares who you are? What can you do? Asmodeus would just kill you, too."

Marcellinus then looked at the man and said, "Then what have you got to lose?"

The man seemed pleased with this answer as he said, "Very well, stranger. I shall tell you. Come with me." The man led Marcellinus and Aloisia to the outskirts of the village and pointed towards the forest as he said, "Do you see that forest? It surrounds the whole village. In order to travel from here to anywhere else, we must travel through this forest. But for about a year now, a terrible beast we call Asmodeus has made that forest its home. All efforts to kill it have failed, for none of the men we sent have returned. Only ones who travel in far enough to see it have come back alive, if they're lucky."

Marcellinus then looked at the man and asked, "What does this creature look like?"

The man then began squinting his eyes and moving his hands about in a strange gesture, as if he were telling a legendary story. "They say it is as big as twenty stone houses and has fangs as long as blades. And they say it has as many arms as an octopus. But the worst part is, they say it even turned the trees of the forest against us. For the tree grabs you and Asmodeus comes to get you and you are never seen again."

Marcellinus just calmly stated, "Do not worry, for this beast shall die by my blade today." With that, he turned to Aloisia. "Come on, Aloisia. We have a monster to slay." She nodded, and they both ran towards the forest.

They reached the edge of the forest and looked upon it. The forest seemed to stretch for miles, with nothing but trees as far as the eye could see. The trees were all a healthy green color as they stood one by one, towering over the pair. As they ventured inside, they soon saw that the shades of the trees made it somewhat dark inside the forest. Marcellinus turned towards Aloisia and said, "Aloisia, stay close to me, for I do not know the dangers that await us." Aloisia, without saying a word, walked close behind Marcellinus. Then they both unsheathed their weapons as they ventured deeper and deeper into the forest. They soon came across a wondrous sight. Every tree was covered in long, white, thick, rope-like substances. Marcellinus placed a hand upon one and realized that it was very sticky. He struggled to get his hand free, but to no avail. He then used his sword to cut through the rope, freeing his hand but getting the sticky rope stuck on his sword. Marcellinus then wiped his sword upon the ground, successfully removing the white, sticky rope. Marcellinus then spoke to Aloisia. "So this is what that man meant by bringing the forest to life." Aloisia then looked up and saw that the white, sticky rope stretched for miles up high in the tree. There was so much that treetops no longer looked green but white. "What kind of sorcery is this?" Marcellinus asked Aloisia.

Aloisia paused for a moment to notice the intricate designs of the sticky ropes, and she told Marcellinus what she thought it could be. "A spider?"

Marcellinus was confused as he turned towards Aloisia. "A spider? What do you mean?" Aloisia then turned to face Marcellinus.

"Yes, look at the intricate designs up there." They both looked to where she pointed and saw a huge design going around and around in a massive circle. "You see, I've seen spiders make very similar designs. They use these webs, as they're called, to catch their prey and drink the fluids within later."

Marcellinus was disturbed by this, as he asked Aloisia, "How do you know so much about bugs?"

Aloisia giggled and said, "I told you, my father taught me many things."

Marcellinus then said, "I see. So if we touch these rope-like things, we will be trapped and will later be food for the beast. Then we'd best avoid them or cut them." So the two began hacking and slashing their way through many webs, cleaning off their weapons every now and then. As they reached the center, they started seeing dried-up carcasses encased in webbed cocoons. Marcellinus approached one and saw the mummified remains of a villager. Appalled, Marcellinus quickly backed away.

In the very center was a massive web, stretching across about six trees. In the middle of it, the two saw a strange object. "What is that?" Aloisia spoke. Unsure, Marcellinus began walking closer to the web. As he did, the object began to move, and he soon saw legs stretching out from it. The object turned itself around, revealing itself to be a humongous spider. "It's Asmodeus!" screamed Aloisia. It was a ghastly beast indeed. The object the two saw was the abdomen of the titanic bug. The titanic spider was round in shape but oddly not completely covered by skin. There were many holes in the abdomen, which seemed torn from the skin stretching. Inside were hundreds of glowing green balls, perhaps eggs. Its back was adorned with massive spikes that stretched from the very back end all the way to the head. The creature had eight beefy legs that each ended with large scythe-like blades, which could easily cut a man in half. The face was hideous to look at. It had a jaw like a human's. The mouth was adorned with massive spiked teeth in two rows, one on top and the other on bottom. It had tiny appendages sprouting from near the mouth as well, which it used to help feed. The beast had two rows of eyes on each side, each having two per row, eight altogether. The eyes were as black as night. The whole body of the spider was a dark gray color, except for the blades of the legs, which were white. It stood at least eighteen tree lengths tall. With a terrifying screech and hiss, the spider slowly made its way down while white spit slopped down to the ground. It touched down on the ground with a mighty roar as the battle began.

Marcellinus yelled at Aloisia, "Aloisia! You cover my left! I will go right!" She nodded as she ran towards the left. Asmodeus was now confused about who to attack as the two warriors slashed at the beast. Unfortunately, its armor skin was tougher than steel.

"Nothing is working!" screamed Aloisia as she jumped and dove to avoid the oncoming slashes of the beast's legs. Marcellinus had no luck either while he swayed and ducked under the spider's blows. Then the two warriors regrouped in front of Asmodeus as the spider screeched and charged towards them. Quickly, the two began to block swipe after swipe of the beast's buff legs. They blocked high and they blocked low, over and over, like a true martial arts display. Then, as they neared a couple of webs behind them, they leaped to the side so as to not get stuck in them.

Marcellinus yelled at Aloisia as Asmodeus tried to regroup to attack once more, "What do we do now, Aloisia?"

Aloisia thought for a couple of seconds and the solution popped in her head. Asmodeus was making another charge towards them while screeching. "Fire!" Aloisia yelled. "I remember my father telling me that spiders hate fire. It will quickly burn their whole web." Hearing this, Marcellinus came up with a plan, but the beast was too fast as it began the relentless attacks once more. The two once again successfully blocked each hit, one by one, until they were forced to roll to the side to avoid the massive web in the middle, where the battle began.

As Asmodeus recovered itself again, Marcellinus took out an arrow and piece of cloth. He then threw it at Aloisia as he said, "Here, take this! Wrap it around my arrow and catch it on fire! Give it to me when it is done! Now go! Hurry! I will keep the beast busy!" Aloisia nodded and ran off to the side. Asmodeus screeched once more as it charged towards Marcellinus. Marcellinus was blocking two arms at the same time in a brilliant display of swordsmanship.

Meanwhile, Aloisia found some sticks and a small rock and quickly started a fire. She then lit the cloth on fire, creating a fire arrow. She yelled at Marcellinus, "Marcellinus! Here, it is done!" Hearing this, Marcellinus quickly rolled backwards while dodging a swipe from the beast. The roll allowed him some distance as he pulled out his bow and caught the fire arrow in his other hand. Very quickly and steadily, he aimed for the glowing green balls of Asmodeus's abdomen. Asmodeus moved in for the kill as Marcellinus released his arrow, and with pinpoint accuracy, it struck one of the green balls, causing it to erupt, and simultaneously caught the rest on fire. Asmodeus was now in a panic as its entire abdomen was engulfed in flames. Each ball was popping out green slime as it erupted. Screeching in terrible pain, the spider hastily climbed back up its web only to have the entire web and the surrounding trees catch on fire. The forest and all the webbing quickly caught on fire, and soon the forest was a blazing inferno. Marcellinus and Aloisia knew they had to clear out or they too would become victims of the fire. As they ran out, they turned to see the flame-engulfed body of Asmodeus running wildly around its web of fire. It didn't take long for its entire body to catch aflame. It was screeching over and over, until finally it stopped and only the sound of cracking wood could be heard as the fire spread more and more. However, as the two made their way out of the forest, as if by some miracle, it began to rain. And in no time at all, the sea of flames was gone and only black smoke and charred trees remained. Marcellinus then spoke to Aloisia. "Come, let's make sure it is dead." They made their way back into the burnt forest and, after a while, came across the burnt body of Asmodeus. It lay there on the ground, very still, blackened from the fire, curled up on its back, almost in the shape of a ball, with its legs pointing inward towards each other. Marcellinus slowly inched his way closer to it.

Aloisia spoke. "Is it dead?"

Marcellinus then used his sword to touch the beast, and with the slightest touch, the beast's body fell apart, turning into nothing but ashes. Marcellinus turned towards Aloisia and said, "Yes, it is dead."

They returned to the village to announce the good news. The same man approached them. "So how did it go? We all saw a huge fire. What happened?"

Marcellinus spoke. "The beast is dead. You can travel once more. All that remains are its ashes."

Hearing this, the man was overjoyed as he led Marcellinus to the same stone stairs they met at before. The man cried out to the people, "Everyone! The great beast Asmodeus is dead! The great warriors, Marcellinus and Aloisia, have bested the beast! Let us celebrate this glorious day!" The village turned into a massive celebration as men, women, and children of all ages were screaming Marcellinus and Aloisia's names over and over. The two warriors felt a bit of a rush for being famous within this village, if but for a moment. *This must be what Emperor Wu feels like*, Marcellinus thought.

The village then threw a massive feast for the two heroes, and they spent the night dancing, eating, and drinking. Each one told the tale over and over of how they slew the beast. Aloisia was a bit sad, however, for she wanted to ask Marcellinus to dance with her, but the chance never came.

They were able to sleep in an inn for the night, in separate rooms. In the morning, they packed their belongings and waved good-bye to the citizens as they made their way out of the village and onto their next stop.

# Chapter 8

After a few more days' journey, the two warriors finally reached the border of China. Marcellinus looked beyond into the new land and spoke. "The border. We are going to be in a new land. Different people who speak different languages." He then looked at Aloisia and spoke. "Are you sure you still want to come? I do not know what awaits us in these new lands."

Aloisia just smiled as she said, "Of course I want to come. I feel safe as long as you're with me."

Marcellinus smiled back and said, "Let us go." And the two traversed into a new land.

After about three days of travel, they came across a small sign written in a strange language. Aloisia looked at Marcellinus, puzzled, for she only spoke Chinese, and asked, "Can you read this, Marcellinus?"

Marcellinus then looked at the sign and turned to Aloisia and spoke. "Yes, it is written in Kazakh. It says 'North is Almaty, largest village in Kazakhstan.' We should continue."

Aloisia then said, "Kazakhstan? I have never even heard of this place. I wonder what the villages and people are like." Marcellinus then looked back at her and shrugged his shoulders, indicating that he had no idea.

Within a day's time, they reached the village of Almaty. Coincidentally, it didn't look much different from the villages of China. All the houses were made of stone, and the marketplace was busy and bustling with people. The food the market sold was much different than anything the two had seen before. They decided to buy some and try it out. They liked most of it, but a few different fruits were most distasteful to them. The people of Almaty also looked so strange to them. The peoples' skin was much darker than Marcellinus and Aloisia's. And most of the men had long, full beards. And almost all the women had strange cloths over their faces, covering all but their eyes. The two didn't receive as many looks as they thought they would, however, perhaps these people had seen travelers before.

As they made their way towards the end of the village, they heard a lot of commotion coming from one of the nearby houses. A large group of people was standing there, screaming and yelling all sorts of things. Since they were speaking Kazakh, Aloisia couldn't make heads or tails of it. But Marcellinus could as he stopped to listen. Aloisia then touched Marcellinus and asked him to translate for her. Marcellinus then leaned over to tell her what they were saying. "The young boy who is crying there keeps repeating that his father was taken by Kun the mighty fish. The other villagers are just complaining about Kun and how they can no longer get fish from the lake. And many people are losing income because fish brings a major profit here."

Aloisia then said, "Kun? If this beastly fish is affecting the lives of these villagers, then maybe we should help, Marcellinus."

Marcellinus then looked at Aloisia, a bit irritated. "Are you sure? Nobody is in any *real* danger. The father of the boy only disappeared because he traveled onto the beast's land."

Aloisia then looked at Marcellinus, dissatisfied. "Marcellinus, it is the right thing to do. Because of this beast, these poor people can no longer enjoy the pleasures and business of fishing—not to mention the many lives it has taken. We cannot allow this to continue."

Marcellinus was still a bit uneasy as he really didn't want to partake in this quest. "Very well, Aloisia. I will see what I can do."

Then the two approached the crowd as Marcellinus began speaking in Kazakh. "People! I am Marcellinus. I am a warrior from China. I have killed many monsters and demons. Please tell me where this beast Kun lives, and I shall destroy it." The people looked at Marcellinus like he was crazy or weird. Marcellinus stood there as the awkward silence continued. Marcellinus spoke again. "Why do you not speak? Tell me where Kun is!"

One man then spoke up, "Why do you want to help us, stranger? What is in it for you?"

Marcellinus then said, "Nothing. I am not looking for any kind of reward. I merely like to help those who are in need, is all. I believe what this beast is doing to your village is wrong, so it must be destroyed."

A bit shocked, the man spoke once more. "I see. If what you say is indeed true, then we will all be most grateful. Kun lives in the nearby lake from which we used to fish. The beast just appeared one day out of nowhere, as if by magic. Some say it is a curse placed upon our village. The lake is north of here, about a day's journey." The man then pointed in the direction of the lake and said, "Good luck; you will need it."

Marcellinus and Aloisia started running towards their destination. Just as the man said, within a day they reached the lake. The lake exterior was quite beautiful, with calm waters and a beautiful assortment of flowers all around, creating a rainbow-like appearance with their many colors. Aloisia looked at Marcellinus and asked, "You can swim, right?" Marcellinus nodded. Then Aloisia continued, "So what is the plan? How do we kill a giant fish?"

Marcellinus said, "I might have to go with my knives, for my sword is too heavy to swing quickly underwater. Your spear will be the same as my sword, so do not use it unless you have to." With that, Marcellinus pulled out two knives, and Aloisia unsheathed her spear. "Are you ready? Then let us go," Marcellinus said as the two jumped into the mighty lake with a splash.

As the two swam down, they noticed the water was a bit foggy, but they could still see pretty well. They both became severely tense as the only sound they could hear underwater was the sound of their hearts beating. As they swam lower and lower, it started to get darker and darker. That's when they saw it: a massive beast slowly swimming towards them. They knew right away that it must be Kun. Kun then spotted the two warriors and, with great speed, swam straight towards them. They both barely missed being chomped by Kun's mighty jaws.

As the beast swam to them in the light, they were able to get a good look at it. The giant fish was as long as two trees and as wide as a whale. The entire body was a greenish-yellow color. Kun's ribs were clearly visible through its sides, which made the beast look more like a skeleton fish than anything else. It had an elongated belly that looked like a growth on its underside. Kun had four massive fins that it used to swim with: two on each side, one on its head, and the other on the tail. Each fin had long spines extending forth, with thin, skin-like membranes connecting from one spine to the next. The beast seemed ages old as it had a strange coral-like beard growing underneath its mouth, which took the vague shape of dead tree branches. Its mouth was as tall as three men and filled with massive razor sharp fangs. This beast could easily swallow a man whole. Kun also had a strange glowing green ball attached to an antenna that connected to the beast's head. It had a gigantic eye the size of two men on each side of its face, emanating a ghostly green color.

As the mighty fish turned around to begin another assault, Marcellinus readied his knives. The fish then let out a growl as it sped towards the two again. Aloisia swam away in time, but Marcellinus tried to get as close as he could to stab the beast. As the fish swam past, Marcellinus missed completely. The fish was just too fast to attack head-on. Marcellinus knew he had to grab the beast and swim with it if he were to have any luck at all in killing it. Aloisia began resurfacing as she was running out of air. Marcellinus, however, stayed below to lure the fish away from Aloisia. As Aloisia was returning to the depths, she saw Kun make a mad dash for Marcellinus, and as the beast neared him, she feared the worst. When the fish swam past Marcellinus's position, she no longer saw him. Aloisia immediately got extremely worried, thinking Marcellinus had been eaten. As the titanic fish turned to face the other direction, she saw Marcellinus hanging onto the side of the fish, hacking away at the beast with his knife, creating an underwater blood cloud, all the while trying to hold on for dear life. Kun was relentlessly growling and shaking madly to try and remove the stowaway from its body. Then it made a dash for the surface, and with a mighty leap, Kun jumped through the air and plunged back into the water in the hopes it would knock Marcellinus off. As the fish flew in the air, Marcellinus took the opportunity to catch his breath. The impact of the splash almost did knock Marcellinus off, but he continued to hold on. After regaining his balance, he began stabbing the beast once more, and blood was pouring out of the wound. Kun decided to make another jump in the air to knock Marcellinus off. When the fish made its way through the air, Marcellinus saw this as a golden opportunity, so he unsheathed his sword and gave the fish a mighty blow to its side, creating a massive cut. The fish was in pain and it splashed back into the water, half-dead, as blood oozed from the wound. Kun was still alive, however, and finally managed to knock Marcellinus off its body. Since the beast was mortally wounded, it could not really swim well anymore, so as Kun sat there, Aloisia swam as fast as she could towards it. With all her might, she swung her spear down towards the fish's head, and it slowly sunk deep into its skull. The beast let out a mighty growl as its movement came to a halt. The blade had reached so far into its skull that one of Kun's eyes popped out and was hanging by a nerve. Aloisia removed her blade as the blood continued to ooze out of its head. The lake was now filled with the beast's blood, making the water red, as Marcellinus and Aloisia watched Kun slowly sink to the bottom of the lake, never to kill any more people. They resurfaced and smiled at each other over a job well done.

They grabbed their belongings they left behind and made their way back to Almaty. As they returned, they were greeted by the same group of people from before, and Marcellinus told them about the entire battle. The people were shocked and couldn't believe the news. Marcellinus assured them that the beast would bother them no more, but the people were not convinced. How did they know that Marcellinus wasn't lying? Marcellinus offered to take them there and prove it to them the next morning after he rested.

The next morning, the group departed, and as they got to the lake, Marcellinus boarded a boat and rode it around the lake for about an hour and proved to the people of Almaty that Kun was dead. Seeing this, they quickly apologized for not believing Marcellinus and they all went back to the village.

Marcellinus realized that people in other countries were not very trusting, and if he were to help any more people, then he decided to bring back a token, or spoils of war if you will, proving his battle wasn't fictitious from now on.

As they returned to Almaty, the people all screamed the good news around the town and they held a mighty festival in celebration of the warriors. After the festival the next morning, the two warriors were getting ready to make leave. When they were leaving, however, a man approached them and gave them a scroll. Marcellinus opened it to see a path leading from Almaty all the way to Syria and then back to China again. The man then spoke. "I heard about your quest to reach Syria and then go back to China, so I wanted to give you this. It is an old scroll that my grandfather made, for he studied geography. I drew a line of the fastest route to get to Syria and then back to China. I hope it helps."

Marcellinus looked at the map, as the path seemed to make a squashed and crooked C shape. He smiled and said, "Yes, this shall come in quite handy, for I do not know this area very well. Thank you very much."

The man said, "No trouble at all. I wish you the best of luck." With that, the two warriors made their way out of Almaty and to the next spot on the map as they waved good-bye to the people.

# Chapter 9

Following the map, Marcellinus and Aloisia arrived in a new country once again; this time they were in Kyrgyzstan. Not long thereafter, they arrived at a medium-sized village named Bishkek, according to the map. The village and the people looked the same as they did in Almaty, but Marcellinus noticed that all the signs were written in a different language. He almost didn't recognize the language, but then he muttered to himself the answer: "It's Russian." Marcellinus realized that Russia must have gained this territory somehow, which would explain the language, he thought.

Marcellinus and Aloisia started slowly walking around the village looking at the many different foods and equipment for sale. They didn't linger around too long and started to make their way out of the village. Marcellinus turned to Aloisia and said, "For once, nothing seems to be wrong. We can just pass through this time."

Aloisia sighed with relief and said, "Thank goodness. No monsters this time."

Suddenly, just as they were exiting the city, an elderly man approached them. He looked highly suspicious; his head and face were completely shrouded in a hood, and he seemed really short as he walked, for he had a hunched back. "Traveling to Talas, huh?" the old man spoke very slowly in Russian. Marcellinus and Aloisia stopped to listen to what more he had to say. "Be forewarned, for the Isha Yaffa will consume your souls!"

Marcellinus asked, "What is this Isha Yaffa, old man?"

The old man spoke once more. "Isha Yaffa is a beautiful angel who patrols the nearby valley. No man has ever made it past her, for her beauty is too grand. Once you look in her eyes, she consumes your soul!" The old man then quickly twitched his head towards the two warriors. "She will consume you too! Ah, ha, ha, ha, ha!" And the old man walked away while laughing hysterically.

Marcellinus spoke to Aloisia. "Crazy old fool. Come on, Aloisia. No monster will stray me from my path, if there even is a monster."

After explaining to Aloisia what the old man had said and exiting the village, Marcellinus ran a bit more until he reached a valley, just like the old man said. Aloisia got a bit worried as she followed behind. "Marcellinus, this is the valley the old man spoke of. Are you sure he wasn't telling the truth?"

Marcellinus was a bit agitated as he said, "Do not worry, Aloisia. Even if there is a monster, we will destroy it together." As the two walked deeper into the valley, they both began to hear a beautiful voice, which started out low but got louder and louder the closer they walked. Marcellinus seemed hypnotized as he said, "What is that beautiful song? The chanting is so peaceful."

Aloisia was then a bit jealous as she said, "It's all right. It's not that great." Marcellinus started walking towards the voice with his eyes wide open and mouth agape. Aloisia saw this and began yelling at him, "Marcellinus! Where are you going? We must go this way! You are going the wrong way!" She sighed and shook her head as she said, "Men." She started to follow behind Marcellinus. It wasn't long at all until they came upon the source of the beautiful song. It was coming from a woman.

The woman was walking in the opposite direction of the two warriors as she continued to sing. Even though they could only see the woman's back, she seemed to be a normal-looking woman. Her skin was as white as snow. The hair looked silky smooth as it flowed gently through the breeze. It was as yellow as the sun. All the woman seemed to have on was a long white gown of sorts that stretched past her feet and halfway down her arms. Just then, the woman turned around to face the two warriors, and her front was just as beautiful as her back. She had very large breasts, and her hair was covering up her face, all except the mouth, and her lips were as red as a rose. She continued singing as the beauty waved her finger towards herself, signaling for Marcellinus to come closer to her. Aloisia was beginning to get upset, as she watched Marcellinus drop his sword and begin walking slowly towards the woman. Aloisia screamed, "Marcellinus! Would you get your act together! Stop drooling over this woman!" But he would not listen as he continued to get closer and closer. Frustrated, Aloisia went over and began to pull on Marcellinus's hand to get him back on track. This upset the singing beauty, and she stuck out her other hand. Suddenly a blast of light shot forth, knocking Aloisia to the ground. Stunned, Aloisia stood to see that the woman had made a drastic change in appearance. Her hair had turned black as the night, and the white gown was now adorned with several rips and holes. Her skin had turned gray like stone. The woman's face was a hideous sight to behold as it finally made an appearance from behind the hair. Her mouth opened very wide, at least seven inches. The teeth were as sharp as knives. And her eyes glowed with a demonic crimson red as she began to cry tears of blood.

Marcellinus still seemed to be hypnotized, so Aloisia knew she had to do something before the Isha Yaffa stole his soul. She tried to strike the beastly woman, but to no avail, as the Isha Yaffa sent another blast towards her, knocking her down once more. Marcellinus was now dangerously close to the Isha Yaffa, so having no other choice, Aloisia ran towards him and pushed him aside, knocking him to the ground. Then Marcellinus rose to his feet, dazed and confused. "What happened? Where am I?" he asked as he looked around. He saw Aloisia on the ground next to him, rising to her feet, as well.

She yelled at him, "Marcellinus! Are you okay? The Isha Yaffa put a spell on you. She almost took your soul!" Marcellinus seemed puzzled and then turned to see the hideous abomination of a woman standing at a distance from him. The Isha Yaffa was now enraged at seeing Aloisia break her spell. The beastly woman rose high into the air and began to emit an ear-deafening shriek. Marcellinus and Aloisia could not bear it as they both collapsed to the ground, covering their ears. Marcellinus tried to fight the noise as much as he could as he returned to his feet, but the Isha Yaffa quickly brought him back to his knees as she began to spin around in circles. Spinning violently in the air, she released powerful shockwaves that knocked him down. Marcellinus realized that if he didn't destroy her, that the terrible shrieking would cause their heads to explode.

With the last bit of his strength, he reached for his bow and arrow, and just before he released his arrow, he said, "Please let my aim be true!" And, as if by magic, the arrow stayed true to his words as it struck the womanly beast clear in the heart. The Isha Yaffa then gasped as her violent spinning came to a halt. The creature looked down as blood started to drip down her white dress. Marcellinus and Aloisia rose to their feet once more as the beast stared at them in shock. The Isha Yaffa began spinning even more violently in the air as she turned into a small tornado of sorts, and, as if by magic, yellow beams of lightning began to strike the tornado. With a brilliant flash of white light, the Isha Yaffa exploded, screaming in agony. After the bright explosion, all that remained was the tattered dress of the beast.

Aloisia smiled and said to Marcellinus, "What would you do without me?"

Marcellinus smiled and said, "Thank you, Aloisia, for saving my life."

She turned and said, "No problem. I guess since I am a woman, the beast's song had no affect on me. Lucky for you I came along, huh?"

Marcellinus just laughed, and then he said, "Come on, we have to keep moving. We should be about halfway to Syria." The two traversed the remaining part of the valley as they continued their journey.

# Chapter 10

Within a day, the two had reached a new village. They were still within the borders Kyrgyzstan. Marcellinus and Aloisia saw a nearby sign, which read in Russian, "Village of Talas." Marcellinus told Aloisia, "According to this sign, we are in a village named Talas. Let us look around for a bit. I am running low on food."

Aloisia nodded as she said, "Okay." As they looked around the different markets, they saw everything but food.

Marcellinus asked one of the vendors, "Excuse me, but where is all the food?"

The man wearily looked up at Marcellinus and said, "The Gigas Vespa came and killed all our cattle and then took off with them."

Marcellinus got irritated as he thought, *Another monster?* He then asked the man about Gigas Vespa. The man pointed him in the direction of the village chief and told Marcellinus to ask there. Marcellinus and Aloisia made their way to chief's house, and Marcellinus knocked on the door. He heard an elderly voice speak, "Come in." The two entered the house and saw an old man standing by a fireplace. He had a medium-sized beard and walked with the use of a cane. The old man spoke. "Who are you? What do you want?"

Marcellinus respectfully answered, "I am Marcellinus. I am a traveler from the East. I had wished to stock up on some food here, but no one seems to have any, and when I asked why, I was sent here."

The old man grabbed his chin as he said, "I see…Well, unfortunately, we have no food to eat, let alone sell, right now. The mighty Gigas Vespa came and slaughtered all our cattle and made off with them."

Marcellinus said, "What about crops? Can you not grow any?"

The old man shook his head, "No, I'm afraid not, for the land is too dry here to grow anything, and it hardly ever rains."

Marcellinus seemed saddened hearing this and asked, "What is this Gigas Vespa, old man? Perhaps I can destroy it."

The old man looked a bit excited, in the hopes Marcellinus would be true to his word, as he spoke. "Gigas Vespa is a giant wasp. It lives south of here, about a quarter of a day's journey. If you are going to defeat this creature, be careful, as people have claimed to have seen more than one. Just keep heading south and you will surely find it." Marcellinus thanked the old man as the two warriors exited the home. He looked at Aloisia and explained the whole story to her.

Afterwards, he asked her, "Aloisia, you are knowledgeable about insects. Please tell me about this wasp, for I have only heard about it and never actually seen one."

Aloisia tried to explain it to Marcellinus. "It is a large insect that closely resembles a bee. Do you know what a bee looks like?"

Marcellinus nodded and said, "Yes, now a bee I have seen."

Aloisia said, "Good, the only difference is the wasp is usually much larger than a bee, and thinner as well. It can sting multiple times and not just once like the bee." Marcellinus looked brain dead as he tried to listen. Aloisia saw this and just shook her head and sighed as she said, "Come on, Marcellinus. Let's just go. You'll see it when we get there."

Then the two began running towards the south, and in no time at all, they came across a graveyard of cattle. There were bones and rotting flesh all around. The smell was truly horrible. "We must be getting close," Marcellinus said to Aloisia. Then the two continued walking, only to stop as they heard the sound of something chewing and ripping flesh. Marcellinus said to Aloisia. "Hide. Something is eating the cattle. It must be the Gigas Vespa." The two quickly hid behind some small bushes. Marcellinus and Aloisia peeked through to see what was eating the deceased cow remains, and then they saw it. The unknown creature then crawled on top of the cow to feast some more. It was a giant wasp, just like the old man had said. The wasp was about as long as two men. It had long, pointy, black legs in the back, two on each side. And two shorter pointy black legs in the front, one on each side. The wasp had long, bulky wings that stretched to almost the size of its entire body. They were a crystal see-through color. Its body was long and thin all the way down to the curving abdomen. From the head to the thorax, it was black. But down the abdomen it had yellow and black stripes going across. The stinger was as long as Aloisia's blade, a solid twelve inches. Its face was rather small, with two appendage-like jaws, which were used to crush meat, and eyes as black as night. The wasp also bore two large black antennae atop its head, which it must have used for smelling various things.

Marcellinus saw this as a golden opportunity to strike as it sat atop the carcass feasting. He quickly pulled out his bow and arrow and, when standing, he shot an arrow, piercing the armor of the beast. With a small screech, the wasp flew backwards from the impact of the arrow and landed on the ground, dead. Aloisia jumped to her feet, smiling and laughing, thinking they had won again, but just as she celebrated, two more Gigas Vespas appeared to attack Marcellinus. "Look out!" Marcellinus yelled as he jumped on top of Aloisia, and they hit the ground to safely avoid the stingers. He spoke to Aloisia. "They must have been feeding, too. We did not see them." The two beasts started to return to kill the two warriors. Marcellinus and Aloisia jumped to their feet and unsheathed their sword and spear, for Marcellinus knew that they were flying too fast for the bow and arrow now.

Aloisia spoke. "I've got the one on the left." Marcellinus nodded as the two wasps flew down to attack. The two had successfully blocked the stingers, and their weapons made a loud clanging sound when they made contact. As the wasps started to fly down towards them again, the two looked at each other and nodded. Just as the wasps flew past them, they quickly traded sides and, with a mighty slash downwards, cut the beasts in two.

Marcellinus said, "Good work, Aloisia. Let us return to the village." Aloisia nodded, and they began to walk back.

All of a sudden, they heard thunderous humming coming from the distance. Marcellinus turned to look at where it was coming from and saw nothing. Marcellinus thought this to be suspicious, so he told Aloisia to follow him as he made his way towards the disturbance. When they neared the center of the disturbance, the humming continued to grow louder and louder. Then that's when they saw it: a gigantic nest of wasps. It stretched for at least ten tree lengths along the ground and was taller than two tree lengths. There was hundreds of holes atop it, leading inside. Marcellinus looked at Aloisia and said, "What abomination is this?"

Aloisia was completely shocked to see such a huge nest. It shined brilliantly with golden hues. She quickly told Marcellinus, "Remember the spider? We must use fire again to burn this nest. There could thousands of giant wasps in there! This is where they live!" Marcellinus pulled out an arrow and wrapped another piece of cloth around it, but as he did, they began to see hundreds of wasp heads poking out of the many holes.

Marcellinus looked at Aloisia and said, "Prepare for things to get bad." They both readied their weapons, as each wasp head screeched, and they all flew out one after the other. Soon the sky was blanketed by giant flying wasps. Marcellinus and Aloisia were in the battle of their lives as they put on a brilliant display of swordsmanship. There was one clang after another as they blocked the hundreds of stingers heading their way. They began chopping and slicing every wasp that they could, and the wasps were dropping like flies. Every time there was a short break, hundreds more would fly out the holes. Marcellinus and Aloisia knew they couldn't survive much longer. Then Marcellinus heard Aloisia scream in pain. One of the wasps sliced her on the back of her leg. She crumpled down on one knee but quickly raised her spear to block the next wasp's stinger. Marcellinus screamed, "Aloisia! Hold on! I am coming!" And like lightning, Marcellinus slashed his way through the two wasps in front of him and made his way towards Aloisia. He killed the wasp behind her from afar with one of his knives. The wasp in front of her was about to sting her in the face. That would end her life. As she stared up at the stinger with tears in her eyes, Marcellinus jumped in front of the wasp and grabbed the stinger with his hands, and with a mighty blow, snapped it in two. Using the sharp end of the stinger, he jabbed the skull of the beast, killing it instantly. He picked up Aloisia, and she reclaimed her spear as the relentless wasp horde kept coming. Aloisia nodded to Marcellinus that she was okay, and with that, Marcellinus said, "Aloisia, can you cover me? I will try to start a fire and end this insanity!" Aloisia nodded as she stood in front of Marcellinus and angrily killed every wasp in her way. Marcellinus grabbed a nearby stone and stick, and as fast as he could, used the stone's sparks to ignite the arrow. He rose to his feet and shot the arrow at a wasp flying in the air. It penetrated the beast, sending the wasp flying into the nest. The arrow pinned the dead wasp against the side of the nest, catching the entire nest on fire. Since the nest was made of a paper-like substance and highly flammable goop, the nest had no trouble bursting into flames. The wasps still inside frantically tried to escape, only to erupt as fireballs and fall flat to the ground. Aloisia and Marcellinus killed the stragglers as they watched the nest burn to the ground with the sound of screaming wasps coming to an end. After the fire died out, Marcellinus walked up to a nearby wasp carcass and, with a quick swipe, beheaded the creature. He picked up the head to bring back to the village as proof of their victory.

The two made their way back to Talas and headed straight for the old man's house. Marcellinus entered without knocking and threw the head of the wasp on the floor by the old man while saying, "There. The deed is done. No more will the Gigas Vespa slaughter your cattle."

The old man was a bit startled at seeing the head on the ground, but he soon spoke. "Really? Oh, thank you, kind strangers! We shall never forget what you have done! Please, is there anything we can do?"

Marcellinus quickly spoke. "If you could provide us shelter for the night and some herbs and bandages to heal Aloisia's leg, I would be most grateful."

The old man looked at Marcellinus with a hearty smile and said, "Of course. It is done." He began to walk out, signaling Marcellinus and Aloisia to follow him. After a short walk, they came upon an inn of sorts. They each had their own room, but Marcellinus stayed with Aloisia so as to help her get in the room.

She started speaking. "Ah. That hurts." Marcellinus realized that walking was beginning to hurt her, as she limped slowly to the bed. Marcellinus came and held onto her and helped her sit down in the bed. Aloisia spoke to Marcellinus. "Thank you. I think my wound is beginning to get infected." A woman entered the room with some herbs and bandages to heal Aloisia's wound.

Marcellinus smiled at Aloisia and said, "Look, here come the bandages. You should be fine now."

Then, as Marcellinus was departing for his room, Aloisia built up some courage and nervously said, "Marcellinus, wait…"

She paused, and Marcellinus turned around as he said, "Yes, Aloisia, what is it?"

Aloisia was blushing uncontrollably, but she took a deep breath and continued. "Would… would you mind helping me with my wound? I…I would feel so much more comfortable if you were to do it."

Marcellinus smiled and nodded and said, "Sure, okay." The woman departed after she handed the herbs and bandages to Marcellinus. Marcellinus sat down next to Aloisia on the bed. He lifted her leg and placed it on his lap. He spoke. "Well first we have to take off your leg armor." Marcellinus paused for a moment as he realized what he was doing. He had never undressed a woman before. For that matter, he had never been around a woman at all before. He looked up at Aloisia's face, and she was blushing and smiling back at him. For some reason, her face seemed to illuminate with beauty in the candlelight, for she was truly a beautiful woman. Marcellinus started to nervously sweat as he unstrapped her armor and placed it on the floor. Then he slowly took off her boot and placed it on the floor as well. He looked up at Aloisia once again, and she was smiling in a very sexual manner. Marcellinus grabbed her other leg and did the exact same thing, even slower than before. Once her armor was off, it was time to take off her under armor on her legs. Marcellinus blushed as he said, "Aloisia? I have to take off your under armor, too." He quickly stuttered as his throat got dry, "I-I can leave if you want me to, so you can take it off in private. Just call me when you're done."

But as Marcellinus was getting up to leave, Aloisia grabbed onto his arm and said, "No, don't go. I want you to do it." Marcellinus saw the lust in her eyes. He was *extremely* nervous now. He sat down once more and began to bring his hand up to her thigh to pull the stocking-like under armor off, and he slowly pulled it down, revealing Aloisia's bare flesh. Her leg was so beautiful as it glistened in the candlelight. Marcellinus just couldn't take it anymore, and he used his hand to grab her naked leg and began to caress it up and down. Her leg was so smooth, like a baby's bottom. Marcellinus began feeling excited; he had never felt this way before. He removed her other stocking, and she turned over to reveal her wound. Marcellinus tried to concentrate as hard as he could on the wound and not her beauty. He quickly ground up the herbs and softly spread it on her wound. Marcellinus placed the bandages on top when he was finished. Aloisia turned back around to face him once more.

Marcellinus seemed like he was caught in a trance, like with the Isha Yaffa, except different. For some reason, this trance felt right. *Could this be how love feels?* he thought. Marcellinus lost control of himself as he neared the angelic face of Aloisia, and said, "Aloisia, I promise to never let anything damage your beautiful body again." She placed her arms around Marcellinus's head, and he got closer and closer until at last they embraced lips in a most heavenly kiss. The feeling was so overwhelming for Marcellinus that he nearly fainted. It was the most pleasurable thing he had ever done. He didn't want to stop, but as soon as Aloisia reached below his belt, Marcellinus quickly snapped out of it and said, "No! I cannot do this!"

Aloisia seemed very sad as she said, "Why? Is…is it me?"

Marcellinus immediately spoke. "No, of course not, Aloisia. You are perhaps the most beautiful woman I have ever seen. I would like nothing more than to make love to you, but my heart belongs to another. For Emperor Wu has commanded that if I complete my journey, I must marry his sister Princess Nangong. I am sorry…I just…I just wish I had met you before my journey; then things would be different."

Aloisia seemed sad, but she was falling in love with Marcellinus, so she quickly recovered and said, "It's okay, Marcellinus. I understand. But I still want to travel with you. I want to help you.

If not as a lover, then as a friend. This Princess Nangong is a lucky woman. I hope she treats you right."

Marcellinus sadly spoke, "Aloisia…"

She smiled and said, "Well, thanks, Marcellinus, for helping me heal. Good night!" Marcellinus smiled back at her and said, "Good night."

He walked out of her room and made his way back to his. On the way, he started to ponder. *Should I refuse Princess Nangong's hand in marriage?* Marcellinus thought. He entered his room and sat down upon his bed and thought, *No I cannot refuse. Disobeying the emperor would bring dishonor to my father.* He grabbed his head as he lay down and thought, *But what do I do? I…I think I am in love with Aloisia. I just want to be with her.* Marcellinus fell fast asleep after crying a tear of frustration.

.

# Chapter 11

The next morning, Marcellinus and Aloisia readied their things to depart, but before they left, the old man approached them and said, "Ah. You have awakened. How was your rest? I hope you found it most relaxing. Before you go, please stop by our shops and take whatever it is you need."

Marcellinus looked at the old man and said, "Thank you for your hospitality. It shall not be forgotten." Then the two went to the shops and grabbed the things they needed. Marcellinus saw they had cattle meat on display now. Since the insects were gone, they were able to bring out the emergency reserves, as new cattle would arrive tomorrow. Marcellinus grabbed all he could carry in his sack, and the two made their way out of the village and onward to continue their journey.

About five days and five nights passed before they reached the next village. On the fifth night, after they stopped to make camp, Marcellinus was staring at the stars once again. Aloisia walked over to him and sat down. Ever since the night in Talas, Marcellinus was a bit nervous around Aloisia. She spoke to him, "So, you ready for your first test?"

Marcellinus laughed and said, "I guess. I hope I do well."

She said, "All right, ready? Which one is that?" She pointed to a cluster of stars that looked like a man holding a bow in his hand.

Marcellinus answered, "Orion?"

Aloisia clapped and said, "Very good, but that one was easy. How about…that one!" She pointed to a group of stars that looked like a V with legs.

Marcellinus paused for a moment, and then he said, "Taurus, I think?"

Aloisia was a bit surprised as she said, "Right again!" She gave Marcellinus a playful evil eye and said, "All right, time for a really hard one!" She looked around for a while and then she pointed to a group of stars that looked like an upside-down horse, in a way.

Marcellinus thought for a while and said, "Wow, this is a tough one. Is it Virgo?"

Aloisia was completely shocked out of her mind as she said, "I can't believe it. You're right. Wow, Marcellinus, you have a great memory." She smiled as she leaned her head on his shoulder. She spoke. "Do you mind if I lay on you and watch the stars with you?"

Marcellinus smiled as he placed his arm around her and said, "Sure. I don't mind."

While she was slowly falling asleep, she said, "You're so warm." Soon, she was fast asleep, and Marcellinus picked her up and carried her to her bed. He gently put her down and pulled the blankets over her. He saw how beautiful she was once again in the moonlit sky.

He reached down and gave her a kiss on the cheek and said very quietly, "I…I love you, Aloisia." He returned to his bed and fell fast asleep.

The next morning, they packed up and continued their journey. They soon reached a village, which, according to the map, was named Jizzakh. They seemed to have entered a new country now, which the map stated was Uzbekistan. They entered the village to see it looking the same as all the others. The people had all looked the same since Kazakhstan. As Marcellinus listened to the people talk, he heard them using a very ancient language, Indo-Iranian. It was a difficult language to understand, so Marcellinus did the best he could. He started to hear stories of a creature called Ba She. From what he heard, the creature was terrorizing the village's economy by swallowing elephants, their main trade item. Upon hearing this, Marcellinus approached a man and spoke. "Man, I am Marcellinus, warrior of China. Please tell me of this beast Ba She."

The man seemed delighted to tell the story once again as he spoke. "Ba She is a terrible monster who lives in the nearby jungle to the north of here. He has been terrorizing our village for many months now. For you see, it eats elephants. We breed elephants to trade to Kazakhstan for money. Lately though, we have had no elephants to trade thanks to Ba She. Our village is in crisis, for we have no money to buy any more supplies."

Marcellinus grabbed the man's shoulder and, feeling bad for him, said, "It will be fine. I shall slay this beast for your village."

The man seemed surprised and asked, "Why? Why are you so nice?"

Marcellinus just smiled and said, "It is the right thing to do." He turned to Aloisia and explained to her the whole ordeal. She just sighed and was a bit saddened, for she was just getting over her wasp wound. Marcellinus then turned to face the man once more. "We will need to borrow an elephant to lure the beast out."

The man nodded and said, "Very well; you may take mine." So, with the elephant, Marcellinus and Aloisia made their way north to the jungle.

It was pretty humid within the jungle, and there were plants and trees covering the ground. They got to a certain point and Marcellinus felt that it was far enough. As he tied the elephant to a nearby tree, he looked at Aloisia and said, "Come on. We must hide and wait for the beast to strike." They hid inside of some bushes, for they were not sure from which direction the beast would come from. They had no idea what to expect, for the man did not go into details, so Marcellinus readied his bow and arrow. After an hour or so, they heard some rustling in some nearby bushes as a loud hissing sound was made. The elephant, sensing danger, was going crazy trying to break free from its bonds. Then slowly, the beast appeared out of the overgrowth of trees and plants. As the beast rose high in the air, Marcellinus and Aloisia realized it was a gargantuan snake. The beast was truly a sight to behold.

From head to tail, it must have been about twenty tree lengths tall. The creature was a solid green jade color from head to toe. The belly was golden yellow. Unlike other snakes, it had a strange line of hair centered on its back, from the tip of its head to the tail. The snake's hair was as black as coal. It also had two horns atop its head, each about six inches long, pointing straight out, not curved like a bull's. The eyes were pitch black, having a thick vertical stripe down the middle. Its mouth was rather large, about the size of one and a half elephants. The beast was equipped with two rows of razor sharp teeth. It also had a forked tongue that constantly spit in and out of the mouth.

As the massive snake was getting ready to strike and eat the elephant, Marcellinus popped up out of the bushes and shot an arrow at the beast. The arrow penetrated the side of the beast. A small amount of blood came pouring out. The snake hissed loudly as it squirmed in pain. Ba She then turned to see its attackers. Forgetting about the elephant, it slithered its way towards Marcellinus and Aloisia. It made a dash to strike the two warriors, but they managed to dodge out of the way as they quickly got up to strike the beast once more. Its body was so long that they still had time to attack as it slithered away. Aloisia gave it a quick slice on its back, and Marcellinus, having unsheathed his sword, also gave it a quick slash on its side. The wounds were rather large, and the snake hissed loudly and swooshed its tail, knocking the warriors down again. This time, Ba She just went straight for Marcellinus. Marcellinus made his way to his feet as the mammoth snake quickly slithered its way towards him, and with its mouth agape, it lunged towards Marcellinus in an attempt to swallow him. Marcellinus, acting quickly, jumped in the air over its mouth and came down with his sword, penetrating the snake through its body, towards its tail end. The sword plunged deep into the ground as well, causing the snake to be pinned down. Trapped, Ba She went into a frenzy and turned to attack Marcellinus once more. Before it could, Aloisia struck the snake with her spear, gashing its side once more. It hissed and turned to attack Aloisia, but Marcellinus pulled out his bow and arrows and began firing the arrows one by one into the beast. Ba She turned to strike Marcellinus, but Aloisia struck it again. Ba She no longer knew who to attack, as every time it turned, the warriors would very badly wound it. Ba She got tired of this and concentrated on breaking free from being pinned. It returned to the ground and began pulling its way off the sword, but Marcellinus ran to the side of the beast and, with a final shot of his arrow, hit the snake in its left eye. Juices from the eye began pouring out as the snake hissed in extreme pain and, with a final mighty tug, freed itself from the sword. But in doing so, it split its body in two from the sword down. It then slowly slithered away and turned around to face our warriors. The jungle floor was now covered in Ba She's blood. The beast had taken quite a beating, but it seemed to want more. About twenty arrows were sticking out of its body, including one in its eye, and it was covered with gashes from Aloisia's spear. The now cyclops snake made another mad dash towards Marcellinus while hissing very loudly. Marcellinus had had enough, however, as he readied his sword. The beast lunged at him with mouth agape, and just as the snake's mouth was going to close around Marcellinus's body, Marcellinus jammed his sword deep inside the snake's mouth, making it go through its mouth and stick out of the top of its head. Marcellinus released his blade as Ba She hissed in pain and twisted and turned high in the air. With a mighty crash, he came to the ground. After the dust settled, Marcellinus and Aloisia approached the snake carcass. The ground had now become a pool of blood. Marcellinus retrieved his sword from the snake and began chopping at its head. After about five slashes, he at last beheaded the beast. Marcellinus dragged the head to the elephant, who was still tied around the tree, and using rope, tied the head to the elephant's body. Marcellinus and Aloisia then hopped atop the elephant and returned to the village.

The two warriors rode back to the village. Once there, the man approached the two warriors and spoke. "How did it fare? I see my elephant survived."

Marcellinus said, "Look behind the elephant and see for yourself." The man looked behind the elephant and saw a long trail of blood connecting to the decapitated head of Ba She. At once the man's mouth dropped in shock. He then smiled and ran throughout the village to spread the word to everyone. Once again, Marcellinus and Aloisia enjoyed a celebratory feast in their honor. They slept at an inn for the night, and the next morning, they headed for their next stop of their journey.

# Chapter 12

It took the warriors seven days and nights before they reached their next destination. Once again, they had traveled into another new country. This time the map said they were in Turkmenistan. The village of their destination was Zakhmet. In a short amount of time, they reached Zakhmet and saw that the village was even more basic than the others, with wooden houses instead of stone. The people looked relatively the same, but dressed a bit differently— nothing that would really differentiate them from the others. As Marcellinus heard them speak, he heard that they spoke another new language. This time it was Turkmen.

As the two made their way through the village, a mysterious hooded man spied on them from afar. When they neared the edge of the village, the hooded man walked up behind them and spoke in Chinese. "Wait! Are you Marcellinus and Aloisia?" Both Marcellinus and Aloisia seemed a bit uneasy as they turned to see a hooded man speaking, for how did he know them?

Marcellinus spoke as he drew his sword. "Why? Who wants to know?"

The man raised his hand, signaling Marcellinus to hold steady. He spoke. "My name is Bartholomew. I have traveled across many countries hunting demons and beasts. I have heard about your exploits in Kyrgyzstan. I have come seeking your aid in destroying a beast that I have chased to this village from Moscow. So will you please help?" The man did look suspicious; he was dressed all in black, with a hood hiding his face, and he wore black gloves.

If a creature was terrorizing people, then he had to help. Marcellinus agreed to help as he sheathed his sword. Bartholomew said, "Follow me. It is not safe out here." They followed Bartholomew inside a nearby vacant house. Once inside, Marcellinus and Aloisia noticed it was home to an abandoned smithy. Bartholomew removed his hood, revealing a middle-aged white foreigner with a full-grown gray beard upon his chin. Bartholomew began to speak. "Thank you for agreeing to help me. This beast is quite dangerous. Its name is Ahriman. It is what my people, the hunters, call a werewolf. For many generations, the werewolf has hunted and killed many people. What's worse, every person the beast bites turns into a werewolf as well. None of my people know the true origins of the werewolf, but I do know they are a dying breed. I have successfully eliminated several werewolves and contained them in one spot in Moscow. However,

52

the leader of this particular pack was Ahriman. He sensed danger, so, leaving his entire pack behind, he fled here. I barely managed to destroy his pack, and chased Ahriman here. As far as I know, he has not bit anyone else since fleeing. However, I am too weak to kill Ahriman myself, for I grow old in my age. Unlike the rest of his pack, who were weak and small, Ahriman is much stronger and bigger. That's why I need you to help me."

Marcellinus was shocked and amazed by the old man's story and said, "If the beast is so powerful, then how can I stop it?"

Bartholomew pulled out a medium-sized chunk of pure silver. "See this?" Bartholomew said. He handed it to Marcellinus and continued to speak. "This is silver. To a werewolf, it is very deadly. Use this silver and this smithy to re-forge your sword, granting you the power to destroy Ahriman. A few slashes to the beast should destroy him."

Marcellinus placed the silver by the smithy and spoke. "This is only enough to forge my weapon; what about Aloisia?"

Bartholomew lowered his head and spoke. "I'm sorry, for this is all the silver I have remaining, and time is of the essence. We have no time to search for more."

Marcellinus was saddened to hear that Aloisia would not be properly protected and said, "Very well. Please give me some time to forge my weapon."

Bartholomew and Aloisia stepped outside. Bartholomew spoke to Aloisia, "I'm sorry that I have no more silver." Aloisia just looked at him, disappointed, and Bartholomew continued, "I shall return in a while. I am going to the shop to restock my supplies." Aloisia watched Bartholomew leave and afterwards walked back inside the smithy to talk with Marcellinus.

Once inside, she saw Marcellinus busily forging his sword using the silver. She desperately asked, "Marcellinus, please let me go with you!"

Marcellinus paused for a moment to speak. "Aloisia, you cannot. You will not be able to hurt Ahriman without silver."

Aloisia began getting more and more upset as she said, "I thought you respected my feelings! I just want to be with you is all! I feel safe when I'm around you! Don't you understand?" A tear began to fall down her cheek.

Marcellinus stopped completely as he slowly walked towards Aloisia. He placed his hand on her face, wiping away her tear as he said, "Yes, Aloisia, I do understand. I want you to come with me as well, but without silver, your attacks will be meaningless. And...and I cannot bear to see anything happen to you." He used his hand to caress her hair as he continued, "You mean too much to me. Please stay here in the village where it is safe. I know you can handle yourself in combat. I mean, you have helped me destroy many monsters, but without silver, you are no match for the beast, thus putting your life in danger."

Aloisia smiled as she grabbed Marcellinus's hand, understanding that he meant no harm with his words. She knew that even if she could fight Ahriman, her attacks would be nothing more than a nuisance to the beast, and if she got bit, she would turn into a werewolf. Feeling a bit better, she said, "All right. I shall stay here, but please let this be the one and only time you leave me behind. I want to face any obstacle with you by my side, head on, no matter the dangers."

Marcellinus smiled and spoke. "I promise. This will be the only time I ask you to stay behind. I feel safer when you are by my side, as well."

Afterwards, Marcellinus continued to forge his blade. In another hour, his sword was finally ready. He lifted his new blade as the silver shined with remarkable splendor. He walked outside, only to see that it was now night. Bartholomew was standing by Aloisia as he confronted Marcellinus and spoke. "Are you ready? It is nightfall, and Ahriman likes to feed at this hour."

 Marcellinus nodded and spoke. "I am ready."

Bartholomew continued, "Good. Ahriman is probably on his way to the village to feed at this very moment, so you must cut him off in the woods. Be careful, Marcellinus, for the beast can see exceptionally well in the dark. Also be sure to avoid his fangs, for one bite and you too will become a werewolf. It is okay to be scratched by his claws, but you must avoid his mouth at all costs, understand?" Marcellinus nodded and made his way to the woods. Bartholomew and Aloisia watched as he vanished into the night. Bartholomew turned to Aloisia and spoke. "Come, let us go inside where it is safe. Do not worry; I'm sure Marcellinus will be fine." Hesitantly, Aloisia followed Bartholomew inside. Meanwhile, Marcellinus was making his way into the forest in the hopes he would find and destroy Ahriman. He could hardly see anything in the darkness of the forest, but luckily clouds moved out from in front of the moon, revealing bright moonlight. Marcellinus was relieved that he could see a little better, but at that same exact moment, he heard a terrible howl from the distance—the howl of a wolf, for sure. Fearing this to be Ahriman, Marcellinus got ready his sword. He heard the sound of running and plants being rustled. As it got nearer and nearer, he could also make out the sound of panting like a dog. Just then, a large dog-like figure burst forth from the bushes in the forest and slammed down to the ground. It rose to its hind legs, and as it howled at the moon, Marcellinus got a very good look at the beast.

It stood tall at about seven and half feet. The beast had the head of a wolf, but the entire rest of its body was that of a man. It was quite a sight to behold. Its head was the exact copy of a wolf, with long, pointy dog ears and a long, pointy snout. The large mouth opened to reveal massive razor sharp fangs. Its eyes glowed with a red evil hue. The head, arms, and feet were the only hairy parts of its body. It was a gray color, making the beast look somewhat elderly. The torso and legs were quite muscular compared to the rest of its body. It had no shirt on, revealing the chest of a human man. The arms and hands were human as well, although the hands were ghastly in appearance, with long, sharp fingernails. Its legs were covered by torn and tattered green pants. The feet, however, were still visible, revealing a weird mutation of a man and dog's foot. It had five toes and was in the shape of a man's foot, but also had an extra toe on the side of the foot just like a dog. The beast also stood on the front part of its feet like a dog. The creature resembled a man even more as Marcellinus saw it bore no tail.

The beast faced forward to see Marcellinus standing there, holding a silver sword, and as drool dripped down the beast's mouth, it began to growl at Marcellinus. Like lightning, the beast charged for Marcellinus, and at the last second, leaped to the right and pounced off a tree and flew towards Marcellinus. Marcellinus quickly turned and slashed his sword, slicing the beast on the arm. It let out a small yelp as it hit the ground. The beast looked at its wound as it was burning with smoke and bleeding, indicating that it really hurt. The sound of heat sizzling from its wound was heard as Ahriman howled once more. The beast realized that only silver could affect it this badly, so it became infuriated. As if by magic, the beast raised its mighty paw-like hands in the air, and with a quick flick of its hands, its fingernails became erect, lengthening to at least four inches long, making all ten as lethal as small knives. Marcellinus got a bit worried as Ahriman made another charge at him, swinging its arms wildly. Marcellinus blocked a swipe to the right, then to the left, then above, then below. The beast was truly quick as it fought with a brilliant martial arts display. Marcellinus continued to block blow after blow from both of the creature's hands, up, down, left, and right. Soon the beast proved to be too quick as it managed to slice Marcellinus in the arm. Marcellinus swung his sword immediately, cutting the beast on the chest. It backed off as its wound began to sizzle, smoke, and bleed. Marcellinus readied himself again. Ahriman made a charging leap at Marcellinus, which he blocked with his sword, but the beast grabbed onto his sword with both hands, and they were now locked in a clashing battle. The beast leaned its head towards Marcellinus as he struggled to keep his sword steady, using all his strength. Marcellinus began weakening, for the beast was just too strong. Ahriman began to make lunging bites at Marcellinus. Marcellinus moved his head to the right, then to the left, as the gaping maw of Ahriman missed him. Drool was flinging left and right onto Marcellinus's face. Marcellinus knew he could not last much longer, so he remembered the battle of the minotaur. As they clashed, he remembered kicking it in the stomach. Marcellinus proceeded to do just that, but the werewolf was too fast. It removed one of its hands from Marcellinus's sword and grabbed his foot. With superhuman strength, Ahriman flung Marcellinus across the forest like a rag doll. Marcellinus was now in an extreme amount of pain as he smashed back first into a tree. A little dazed, he quickly regained his sword as the beast ran towards him to finish him off. It made a mighty leap in the air as it plunged downwards towards Marcellinus. Marcellinus, with a mighty slash, sliced the beast across the belly. The beast fell to the left, to the ground, and let out a loud yelp as it shriveled on the ground in pain. Marcellinus recovered to his feet as he approached the body of Ahriman on the ground. The beast seemed dead, but Marcellinus saw it still lightly breathing. He readied his sword in an attempt to destroy the beast, but as he approached Ahriman, it shot up from the ground like lightning for one final attempt to kill Marcellinus. Marcellinus, reacting too quickly for the beast, plunged his sword deep into the beast's skull. Ahriman dropped to the ground and instantly died. Marcellinus wiped the sweat from his brow as he recovered his sword from the beast's carcass. He dragged the lifeless body back to the village.

He noticed that it was really late in the night now, for the village seemed empty. He proceeded to the abandoned smithy, where he knocked on the door. Bartholomew quickly answered the door and saw the injured Marcellinus standing before him. As he looked behind Marcellinus, he saw the dead body of Ahriman. Bartholomew spoke. "My word. I can't believe you actually did it. Well done, Marcellinus! Well done!" Bartholomew proceeded outside to check on Ahriman's body.

Marcellinus entered the house. He saw that Aloisia was resting. He gently woke her up and spoke. "Aloisia, I have returned. The beast is dead."

Aloisia immediately hugged Marcellinus as she was happy to see him alive. She spoke. "Oh, Marcellinus! I was so worried about you!"

He hugged her back and spoke, "I am fine. The beast scratched me, but I managed to avoid its fangs."

She was just relieved that Marcellinus was okay as she began to speak once more, "That's great! I'm so proud of you."

Then the two stopped hugging as Marcellinus spoke. "Well, it is pretty late, and I still have a journey to complete. I should get some sleep." Aloisia just smiled as she wished him a good night's rest.

As Marcellinus made his way to his bed, he noticed Bartholomew dragging the carcass of the werewolf into the house. Bartholomew spoke. "Don't mind me, Marcellinus. I am just going to prepare the beast for some tests I will run on him in the morning." Marcellinus nodded as he crawled into the bed and fell fast asleep.

The next morning, he was awoken by Aloisia, who spoke. "Marcellinus, Bartholomew wanted me to wake you up." Marcellinus grabbed his things and made his way to the front door. Aloisia followed as she was already ready to go. As they approached the door, they saw that Bartholomew was no longer inside, so they walked outside. Outside they saw that Bartholomew was on the back of a horse with the dead body of Ahriman wrapped up in many cloths, keeping it hidden from view.

Marcellinus spoke. "Leaving, Bartholomew?"

Bartholomew looked at Marcellinus and spoke. "Yes, my friend. I must return to the hunter headquarters so they can examine Ahriman's body more clearly. Perhaps we can find a cure for the werewolf bite or even more affective weapons. It's all thanks to you, my boy!" Marcellinus smiled at Aloisia, who smiled back. Bartholomew smiled as he looked at the two of them and said, "Well, I must be going. Good luck, you two; I hope you are able to complete your quest." With that, Bartholomew kicked the side of his horse while yelling, "Hyaah!" Marcellinus and Aloisia watched as he rode off in the distance, knowing that they would probably never see him again. Then the two warriors began their journey once more.

# Chapter 13

After another five days and five nights, the two found themselves in another new country, the country of Iran. They noticed this place was very hot and mostly surrounded by deserts. It was difficult to travel through the desert due to the extreme heat, but the two managed to get to their next town, which, according to the map, was a village named Mashhad. People here looked much different than in previous countries. They all wore turbans upon their heads and light cloth clothing all over their bodies. The women, however, still covered their whole bodies except their eyes. The men's beards seemed much longer than in the other countries as well.

As Marcellinus walked around, he heard a new language being spoken. After hearing it for a few seconds, he recognized it as the Persian language. As the two walked by the markets, they heard a lone woman crying. Marcellinus and Aloisia approached her as Marcellinus spoke. "Woman, what is wrong?"

The woman wiped away her tears as she looked up at Marcellinus and said, "Ghayb…Ghayb killed my husband." Then two other villagers came to comfort the woman as they picked her up to her feet.

As they helped her walk away, Marcellinus screamed at one of the villagers, "What is Ghayb? What has happened to her?"

The villager let go of the woman only for a second to answer Marcellinus's question. "Ghayb is our curse. If you want to know more, ask Habib."

Marcellinus pondered as to who or what Habib was. He decided to ask around to see if anyone knew of Habib. He approached a man walking and spoke, "Excuse me, can you tell me of Habib?"

The man looked at Marcellinus and began to speak. "Habib is the village elder. He lives over there." The man pointed to a rundown stone house in the distance. Marcellinus thanked the man as he and Aloisia made their way to Habib's house.

Marcellinus knocked on the door, and an elderly man walked from around the corner of the house on the outside. He was dressed like the other men, and he was still able to walk upright, which was shocking given his age. The man spoke. "Who are you? A traveler?"

Marcellinus nodded. "Yes, my name is Marcellinus. I hail from China. Are you Habib, the village elder?"

The old man nodded as he spoke. "Yes, I am Habib. What can I do for you?"

Marcellinus began to explain about the woman. Afterwards, he asked, "So I was wondering if you could tell me about this Ghayb."

Habib told the two to come inside and he would tell them all he knew. As Marcellinus and Aloisia entered, they saw Habib's house was quite simple in appearance and was only big enough for two people at the most. Habib asked, "Before I tell you of Ghayb, please tell me why you are interested."

Marcellinus spoke, "I have traveled very far and have overcome many hardships. In my travels, many people have been in danger. As a warrior, I feel it is my duty to help people."

Hearing these words, Habib smiled and talked some more. "Oh, I see. Well perhaps you can help. Hold on for a second." Habib approached his bed, and as he reached underneath it, he pulled out a book. After blowing off the dust, Habib opened it as he began to speak to Marcellinus. "This book is a journal kept by my grandfather. It is quite old, and it explains the origin of Ghayb. It says here that long ago, when my grandfather was leader of this village, in the nearby mountains in the desert, an evil witch had made her home. No one knows where the witch came from or why she was evil. One day, she came to the village looking for some food, but as she approached a vendor to grab some, the merchant asked if she had money to purchase the food. She did not have any, and the merchant quickly hollered aloud that the old woman was a thief. Hearing this, my grandfather approached the merchant and old woman. My grandfather tried to calm down the merchant who wanted the old woman's hand to be severed as penance for stealing. My grandfather was a gentler man, and he politely told the old woman that she needed money to purchase the food. This made the old woman angry, and she floated high in the air, revealing herself to be a witch. She used powerful magic to summon a portal from another dimension. As the portal remained open, she started to chant a weird spell. The spell caused an evil spirit to appear, which we call the Ghayb. It immediately attacked the merchant, dragging him inside the dimension, never to be seen again. My grandfather immediately ran back to his home and grabbed a spear. As he returned, he noticed the Ghayb was pulling everyone it could into the abyss. The witch was still floating high in the air, continuing to chant. My grandfather released the spear, and it struck the witch, killing her instantly. She fell back to the ground, motionless. As she lay dead, the Ghayb also became motionless. Although the beast did not disappear, my grandfather approached the body of the witch. As he neared her body, he realized she was still alive, as her chanting continued, and like magic the witch's body disappeared, leaving only her clothes behind. Suddenly, the Ghayb activated once more, but only to disappear back into the portal. Ever since that day, the Ghayb appears once a day to drag a person into its abyss, but it is not always successful. We have only lost about five people in six months. We have learned to be better prepared now, but we shall never know peace until this foul beast leaves us forever."

Marcellinus and Aloisia were both now resting on chairs, and Marcellinus spoke. "If it is a spirit as you say, then how can we kill it?"

The man looked at Marcellinus and spoke. "That is the problem, for one cannot kill something that is already dead. We have tried many things, and physical attacks only make it madder. And we tried using holy weapons blessed by the prophets of Bethlehem. Still nothing has worked."

Marcellinus looked puzzled as he knew not what to do. He asked Habib, "What more can you tell me about the witch?"

Habib continued, "Well some say the witch transferred her soul to within the Ghayb, while others believe that the Ghayb is her shadow and she lives within the dimension, controlling its every move."

Marcellinus had an idea, and he told Habib, "Gather everyone in the village to the center of town. With everyone gathered, the beast is sure to make an appearance."

Habib seemed worried by this as he asked, "Why? What is your plan?"

Marcellinus spoke. "Just do it."

Habib still seemed uneasy as he continued, "But the Ghayb has already appeared today. What makes you think it will return?"

Marcellinus snapped back at Habib, "Habib, just go! It is impossible for the beast to ignore the village grouped up in such large numbers. It will come to steal many people, and when it does, I shall destroy it!" Hearing Marcellinus getting angry, Habib exited the house and began yelling at the villagers to meet in the center of town.

As Marcellinus and Aloisia exited the house as well, Aloisia turned to Marcellinus and asked, "Marcellinus, what is going on? What are we doing?" Marcellinus felt bad, for he forgot that Aloisia could only speak Chinese. He apologized to her as he told her the entire story about the Ghayb and what it does.

Marcellinus told her his plan. "And my plan is, once I gather everyone in the village, the Ghayb should appear. When it does, I shall jump into the dimension it creates, for I believe the witch still lives inside and is controlling it from there. I believe she stays alive by feeding on human souls, much like the Isha Yaffa did."

Aloisia looked worried as she spoke. "But, Marcellinus, it's too dangerous! What if you get trapped inside the dimension?"

Marcellinus smiled and said, "Do not worry, Aloisia, I will escape. The dimension will stay open as long as the Ghayb thinks it can steal souls. As soon as I kill the witch, I shall make haste for the exit. Aloisia, I need you stay outside and protect the villagers, understand? I am counting on you. Do not let that beast steal any souls."

Aloisia still seemed uneasy as she answered, "Okay, I will do my best."

Finally, Habib gathered all the townspeople in the center, and he then approached Marcellinus and said, "I have done what you asked. Now what do I do?"

Marcellinus responded, "Just try and keep your people calm, for the Ghayb shall surely appear soon." Habib walked back to the people and began to talk to them and comfort them. In no time at all, the sky grew dark and a monstrous screech was heard in the distance. Marcellinus looked at Aloisia and said, "Get ready! Here it comes!" They both rushed to the center, where the people were gathered. Then, with a flash, a large portal appeared. It was in the shape of an oval as it hovered there, twirling around and around. It had a strange black and purple color to it.

People began to scream, "The Ghayb is here!" and they started to run for shelter. Habib tried to keep everyone together, but it wasn't working out too well. Then a figure slowly appeared through the portal. Making a full appearance, it cried out with a terrible shriek and began flying towards the running people.

The Ghayb was really not much to look at. It was transparent, giving off a ghostly aura. The specter wore a black cape all over its body. The ghost only bore a head and arms, and neither legs nor feet were visible. Its arms were just as black as the cape, ending in long, sharp fingernails. The face, however, looked just like a human skull, and it bore red demonic eyes. The Ghayb flew slightly above the ground, moving to wherever it needed to go in quite a hurry. It was also able to pass through walls and doors. The specter was the size of a normal man, and the cape flowed around in the wind but looked rather old as it was ripped and torn in several places.

As the Ghayb flew towards a group of running civilians, Aloisia ran towards them to aid them. Aloisia approached the ghost. She tried to slice it with her spear, only to see it pass straight through its body. The Ghayb turned to face Aloisia and screeched loudly as it began to chase her. Aloisia tried her best to fight it off, but nothing worked. She ran for safety with the beast closing in behind her. Aloisia was saved, though, as it sped towards a group of people running back to their homes, giving chase to them. Aloisia would run up to Ghayb and slash at it with her spear to get its attention. The beast would then begin to chase her, as she would run for cover. Ghayb would then spot more people and chase them, just like before. Aloisia would continue to play this game of cat and mouse in the hopes Marcellinus would defeat the witch.

Meanwhile, Marcellinus had embraced his courage as he jumped through the portal. He was in a strange place, as it was completely colored red. The walls, ceiling, and floor were all red, and it seemed to be somewhat wet and dripping. *Blood perhaps?* Marcellinus thought as he walked though the slimy mess. Shocked at believing the room to be covered in blood, Marcellinus walked a bit more to see the figure of the witch floating in the air on top of a small red hill of sorts. He got a good look at her, and she was just as the book described. She wore old ragged clothing. Her hair was gray, long, and pointing out in sharp ends as it flowed in the wind. The witch's skin was very pale, with small cracks all along it. Her teeth were disgusting, as they had turned green and yellow. The witch's eyes were as white as the moon.

She spoke with a cackling voice, "You are not welcome here!" She lowered her hand, and lightning was released from her fingertips. Marcellinus quickly leaped out of the way as the witch continued her barrage of lightning bolts. Marcellinus began running off to the side as he readied his bow and arrows. The witch halted the lightning and began to chant, and suddenly the floor beneath Marcellinus sunk, causing him to be trapped. The witch spoke, "Now I shall feast on your soul!" Just as the witch was about to strike the final blow to Marcellinus, he raised his bow and quickly shot off his arrow, piercing her chest. She screamed very loudly as she fell to the floor in pain. The witch seemed to have lost her concentration, as the floor beneath Marcellinus returned to normal once more. With quick and effective precision, Marcellinus ran towards the witch, who was desperately trying to remove the arrow, and sliced her across the stomach with his sword. As she leaned back and screamed, Marcellinus raised his sword into the air and, with a final blow, impacted her skull, splitting her face in two. The screaming came to a halt as her own blood now littered the floor, for she now laid there motionless. The room began to shake and crumble apart, as the very essence keeping the room together had been destroyed. Marcellinus knew he must make haste for the exit before he became the Ghayb's final victim.

Meanwhile, outside, the Ghayb was closing in on Aloisia. She thought she was done for, but the Ghayb stopped in midair as flashes of light started to break through its body, like spears. With a final screech, the beast exploded in a bright flash of light, never to be seen again. The portal also disappeared just as Marcellinus leaped from its mouth back to safety.

The villagers began to cheer as their nightmare had finally come to an end. Habib ran towards Marcellinus, laughing and cheering as he said, "Thank you, my friend! Thank you! Now we can live at peace once more!"

Aloisia ran to Marcellinus and wrapped herself in his arms. She said, "I'm so glad you're safe. I was worried about you. I did my best to hold off the Ghayb. Luckily, nobody was killed." Marcellinus smiled as he hugged her back, saying how proud he was of her. Habib then announced to the villagers that they would have a grand feast in the warriors' honor. Like many times before, the two feasted and drank to their hearts' content as they told the tale of defeating Ghayb over and over again.

By morning it was time for them to go, as Marcellinus still had a quest to complete. They waved good-bye to Habib and the villagers as they made their way out of the village.

# Chapter 14

After seven days and nights, the two reached their next village, the village of Tehran. Still being in Iran, the people and village looked virtually the same as in Mashhad. Tehran seemed a bit bigger, though. The only thing that Marcellinus and Aloisia noticed was the sight of people rebuilding their homes, which seemed odd for many people to do all at the same time. The two were nearing the edge of the village and felt a bit relieved as they heard no cries of help whatsoever. As they walked, they suddenly heard a man scream, "It's Jahannam! Jahannam has returned!" Marcellinus and Aloisia turned to see a massive bird engulfed in flames approaching the village as it screeched loudly, sounding like an eagle.

It was truly a remarkable sight, for the entire beast was covered in red, orange, and yellow flames but still held onto the shape of a bird. The firebird was about two tree lengths tall. Its tail stretched far behind its back as it stuck out in a point. Jahannam's feet extended in mighty flame talons. Its wings were quite impressive as it flapped them back and forth very slowly. The beast's head was small, and the mouth ended in a large point of flame. Its eyes shined with a beautiful blue, like the color of the sky. As Jahannam moved, flames danced around its body, as some would depart from its body into the sky, just like real fire.

It swooped down at the village and began spewing forth mighty flames, burning many villagers and setting the stone houses on fire, turning the stone black as it was charred. Marcellinus and Aloisia barely escaped the flames as they rolled to the side. As the beast turned around to continue its assault on the village, Marcellinus readied his bow. He shot the beast four times with arrows, but the arrows quickly burst into flames as they neared its body. It began to spew forth flames once more as it swooped down again. Marcellinus and Aloisia rolled once more. Then, as quickly as it appeared, the beast disappeared. Everything seemed peaceful now as the villagers dragged the burned carcasses off to the side and started putting out the flames with water. Marcellinus looked at Aloisia and spoke. "Aloisia, we must do something to help these people."

Aloisia nodded as she said, "You're right. But how do we stop a beast made entirely of fire?"

Marcellinus thought for a second and then he spoke. "Perhaps if we were to throw water at it somehow."

Aloisia said in disbelief, "It would take a whole lot of water to kill that beast."

When Aloisia said this, it gave Marcellinus a brilliant idea. He turned with excitement to Aloisia and said, "A pool of water! That is the answer! I remember the map saying there was an oasis not far from here. If we rally the villagers together, we can spend the day digging a massive hole in the middle of town and have the rest travel to the oasis and gather all the water they can. We fill up the hole with water and cover it up somehow, so when the beast returns, it will swoop down and land in the water, killing it."

Aloisia was amazed to hear such an elaborate plan and spoke, "Wow, Marcellinus, how did you think of building a pool of water? That is very creative."

Marcellinus blushed as he spoke. "Well you kind of helped me think of it, by mentioning the fact that we would need a lot of water. So I thought of how we could get all that water in one spot."

Marcellinus blushed even more as he rubbed his head. Aloisia laughed as she spoke. "Hee, hee, hee. Cute, a great fighter, and smart. Looks like I picked the right guy to be around."

Marcellinus smirked. He made his way towards the town as he spoke to a group of villagers, telling them of his plan to defeat the beast. One man spoke up. "But if we use the water from our wells, we will die of thirst."

Marcellinus shook his head and said, "No, there is an oasis a half a day's travel from here, due north. We send everyone we can there to pick up water and bring it back here." The man thought it was a good plan, but not everyone would go for it. Marcellinus pleaded with the man to try and convince everyone he could.

The man did agree but made no promises. The man came back after a while with only a handful of people and said, "Sorry, but people either think I'm crazy or they're too scared. These are the only people I could get."

Marcellinus got angry and walked towards the center of the village and yelled, "My name is Marcellinus! I am a traveling warrior hailing from China! I have volunteered to defeat the beast Jahannam! Are you people not tired of being tortured by this beast?! I ask you, no I implore you, to help me build this pool! I swear to you it shall work! I have traveled far and slain many beasts! So I ask, who has enough courage to step forward and help me reclaim your lives?!" Everyone just stood there for a while, staring at Marcellinus with broken eyes and spirits. But then one man stepped forward and grabbed Marcellinus on the shoulder with a smile. The others embraced their courage and walked forward as well, and soon the entire village was standing around Marcellinus. Marcellinus yelled, "Death to Jahannam!" The people all began to cheer with excitement.

Soon, many people gathered around Marcellinus with shovels, as the others went with Aloisia on loaded donkeys to travel to the oasis. Marcellinus and the others quickly began to dig in the heat of the scorching sun. Aloisia and her group shortly reached the oasis and began loading buckets and chests of water, one by one. Once each was finished, the oasis almost seemed bare.

Nightfall was approaching as Aloisia and her group returned to Tehran. Upon their arrival, they noticed that Marcellinus and his group had built a big hole that was one tree deep and three trees long. Then, one by one, the people and Marcellinus climbed the ladder, exiting the hole. They started pouring the water into the hole, and within no time, the water filled it about halfway. Marcellinus nodded and said, "This is good enough. Now we need something to hide the hole from Jahannam until it attacks again." Then, one by one, the villagers began to bring out all the rugs and animal blankets they could, and they began to cover up the hole, until at last it was completely covered.

Exhausted, Marcellinus and Aloisia began to walk to the house that one of the villagers had kindly offered them to stay at for the night. But there was only one room for them, which meant that Marcellinus and Aloisia would have to spend the night together. They entered the room together, and Marcellinus and Aloisia placed their weapons on the ground. Marcellinus readied his bed and began to take off his sack. He turned around and noticed that Aloisia was getting undressed. She already had one leg of armor and one boot off. Marcellinus blushed as he panicked and turned back around to face the wall. He slowly made his way to the door as said, "I am sorry. I shall leave until you are undressed."

Aloisia laughed and blushed as she said, "Oh no don't worry. I really don't mind." Marcellinus stopped and turned around to face her for only a second and then made his way back to his bed, saying, "All right. Good night, then."

Aloisia smiled and said, "Good night." Marcellinus crawled into bed and closed his eyes, but he was not asleep, for the temptation to watch Aloisia undressing was too strong. So he opened his eyes a tad so as to keep Aloisia from noticing him spying. As he watched her undress, he got nervous and sweaty with anticipation. He lay there and pondered how someone as beautiful as Aloisia could even exist. Her beauty was truly unmatched and was equal to an angel's. The light of the candle seemed to add a glowing and beautiful hue to Aloisia's soft body. She had now taken off all her armor and her leg under armor, leaving her upper and waist under armor still on. She slowly unwrapped her silky smooth hair from her ponytail. She waved her hair sensually through the air as time seemed to slow down. Marcellinus's eyes shot open and got huge as he watched her standing there. Glowing in the candlelight, her smooth legs begged to be rubbed and caressed. His eyes moved up to her chest and then to her beautiful face. Marcellinus wanted to kiss every inch of her body. She crawled into bed, after blowing out the candle, and turned the other way, opposite of Marcellinus. Before she fell asleep, she smiled as she rolled her eyes towards Marcellinus as if she knew he was watching her undress. Marcellinus's eyes were open and wide, still unable to get over her beauty. He then rolled over to try and get some sleep.

The next morning, Marcellinus awoke to find Aloisia gone. He exited the house only to find her waiting for him. She laughed and spoke, "Good morning! How did you sleep?"

Marcellinus smiled and said, "I slept fine."

She gave him a smirk and said, "Were you watching me undress last night?"

Marcellinus blushed and cringed when he heard that question, and immediately answered, "N-no! Of course not! I hit the bed and fell right to sleep!"

Aloisia cringed and squinted her eyes as she said, "Hmm…"

Just then, a man screamed, "Jahannam! Run and hide! Jahannam has returned!" People began to rush indoors as Marcellinus and Aloisia made their way in front of the pool of water they made. As the monstrous bird swooped down, it once again spewed forth flames, burning the village.

As it neared them, Marcellinus spoke to Aloisia. "I must get it to swoop down towards me!" With that, Marcellinus gave Aloisia one of his knives as he held another. He spoke. "Let us throw these. They will not melt like arrows. And perhaps it will make the beast fly to us!" Afterwards, they both threw the knives in the sky, striking the beast. It somehow seemed to affect the beast, as it screeched loudly, directing its attention towards Marcellinus and Aloisia. Angrily, it swooped down, attempting to capture them both in its flamed talons. Marcellinus and Aloisia waited until the very last moment before they jumped to the side. Once they did, the mighty bird flew straight into the hidden pool of water. With a loud and terrible hiss, the flames died out. Smoke and haze now filled the air, making visibility difficult. Marcellinus knew the beast had not died, for the sound of screeching could still be heard. As the smoke and haze cleared, Marcellinus could see the body of a regular bird in the water. It was gray from head to toe. The bird still had blue eyes. It was splashing and struggling within the now empty pit, for its wings were still too wet to fly. Marcellinus quickly hopped down into the hole with his sword drawn. The titanic bird began thrashing around, trying to peck Marcellinus as he slashed its side over and over again. The beast was now bleeding very badly. As it screeched in pain and struggled to its feet, Marcellinus delivered a mighty blow to its neck, decapitating it. Blood oozed onto the ground. The villagers rushed over and dropped the ladder down to Marcellinus, and he quickly climbed out. The villagers began to cheer as Aloisia ran to Marcellinus, giving him a big hug.

The town celebrated with loud cheering and much feasting. Since it was still morning, Marcellinus and Aloisia knew they had to continue on their way. The villagers all thanked the two warriors, saying they would never forget what they had done to restore peace to their village. They waved good-bye to their new friends. Marcellinus and Aloisia made their way out of the village and onward to their next stop.

# Chapter 15

After three days and nights of travel, Marcellinus and Aloisia reached their final destination in Iran, a village that was called Kermanshah. Settled near the desert, the village was not very different from the rest of the villages in Iran. The people all seemed to dress the same and lived in similar stone houses. Marcellinus and Aloisia walked along the grassy but sandy road ahead. They decided to take a quick rest in the shade of the merchants' tents to cool off from the burning sun. Marcellinus pulled out his map and flung it open. Upon inspection, he smiled and said to Aloisia, "Look, Aloisia. We are nearly there! Syria is not far from here at all!" Aloisia just smiled in return. He put the map away and, with excitement, began to walk forward out of the village. As they approached the exit, a woman and man came running into the village. They were screaming wildly as tears rolled down their eyes. It took a couple of minutes before Marcellinus could make out what they were saying.

"The Fajarah! The Fajarahs have our son and daughter!" Marcellinus told Aloisia that something was wrong as the two hastily moved towards the two weeping parents. They pushed their way through the crowd of villagers until they got to the front. They heard the father talk as he held the crying mother. "We were trying to travel to Iraq, but as we reached the border, the Fajarahs came and took our children! We have no weapons to fight back. Please, can someone help our children?"

The entire group of villagers fell silent, as they looked at each other, thinking this task to be suicide. Immediately, Marcellinus stepped forward and spoke. "I am Marcellinus. I am a warrior from China. I will save your children!"

The man and woman looked up at Marcellinus with kind and loving eyes as the man said, "Thank you, kind stranger! They must have taken them to their home in the desert! Please, you must save them!"

Marcellinus nodded as he asked, "I will. But please tell me, what is a Fajarah? And where do they live?"

The man continued, "A Fajarah is a flying demon. Their numbers are great. They have made their home in some ancient ruins within the desert. They have been there since ancient times. We thought we would be safe if we just went around them. But we were wrong." The man pointed west of the village as he continued to speak. "Go this way. The ruins are close to the border." Marcellinus turned to Aloisia as he told her everything that was happening. Understanding the situation, they wasted no more time and ran out of the city and towards the ruins that the man had spoken of.

In a half a day's journey, they reached the ruins. The ruins were old and decrepit. The limestone color had tarnished and faded away over time. None of the parts of the buildings were even recognizable, as they were buried deep into the sand. Small vines and shrubbery had wrapped themselves around the parts that still existed above ground, adding to the age. The largest building was in the center and a hole was carved deep into the sand in the middle of the building.

At first there was no sign of the Fajarahs, but hearing a fierce growl, the two looked up to see two massive flying beasts approaching them from above. As the creatures stopped and hovered in midair to angrily growl at Marcellinus and Aloisia, the two got a very good look at the beasts. They stood about seven feet tall. Their entire bodies were blacker than the night sky as the eyes glowed a bright jade green. They seemed to have the bodies of men. The wings stretched long behind their bodies, at an impressive four feet for each wing. The skin-like membranes of the wings were the only lighter part of their bodies as they bore a grayish color. The wings each ended with long points, with a lone claw atop each wing. Each of the five fingers of their hands bore mighty talons long enough to wound deeply. Their feet were fashioned with two toes in the front and one in the back. The two in front were separated by a grayish-colored membrane. Although the beasts were not very muscular, their mighty tails more than made up for it, as the tails were quite wide and buff. They stretched a good six feet behind the beasts, ending in a sharp, pointed arrow, like true demons. Their faces were ghastly, as they had two long, pointy ears that were about seven inches. The actual faces resembled a dog's in some ways. The nose stuck out like a dog's. When opening their gaping jaws, the beasts revealed two rows of razor sharp teeth with a long snake-like tongue.

After hovering for a while, the two Fajarahs swooped down to attack Marcellinus and Aloisia. Drawing their weapons, they got ready for combat. As each beast swayed back and forth to attack with their mighty slashes, Marcellinus and Aloisia swung their weapons. In no time at all, they had dealt a deadly blow to each beast's chest. The beasts both fell to the ground, dead, as blood poured from their wounds. They approached the dead carcasses as Marcellinus spoke. "What a truly foul beast. It really does look like a demon."

Aloisia hesitated and spoke, "I...I think it's a gargoyle."

Marcellinus looked at Aloisia with a puzzled face as he spoke. "Gargoyle? What is that?"

Aloisia spoke once more, "Well, like many other things my father taught me, he also taught me of many demons that my great-great-grandfather and great-grandfather saw during their travels. They each wrote pages about the demons they came across and fought. My father showed me the books several times, and I remember seeing this particular beast in the book of my great-

great-grandfather. He wrote of how he slew many of these beasts. He drew the pictures in his book, which look exactly like this beast. He called them gargoyles. They are supposedly a low-level demon from the underworld." Marcellinus was both shocked and impressed at Aloisia's vast amount of knowledge. She truly was a one-of-a-kind woman.

Marcellinus spoke, "If these truly are demons, then we must hurry to rescue the children, for demons have been known to eat the flesh of man, according to my father."

The two then made their way to the large buried building in the center. As they approached, they heard more growling, and about ten more gargoyles appeared from the hole. Marcellinus and Aloisia readied their weapons as they prepared for a mighty fight. In a seemingly intelligent fashion, the beasts split into groups of five, as five flew to Marcellinus and five flew to Aloisia. The two warriors began swinging their powerful sword and spear, as one by one the beasts fell to their death. Just as the battle ended, the two looked up to see the sky was now littered with nearly eighty of the terrifying beasts. Marcellinus and Aloisia stood side-by-side as, one after the other, the beasts dive-bombed to attack the warriors. Marcellinus and Aloisia successfully blocked attack after attack of the ferocious demons' claws. They would immediately retaliate with a quick slash to the chest or face, killing the beasts. After a while of killing, there were only about twenty left. Unfortunately, Marcellinus and Aloisia were quickly growing tired. As Marcellinus looked up, he noticed the final twenty were just hovering there in the air. He turned to Aloisia and spoke. "Have they given up? Did we win?" Aloisia just looked at him with tired eyes as she knew that was not the answer. Suddenly, they both began to feel the ground shake as a titanic hand appeared out of the hole and slammed down to the ground. Within seconds, another hand had appeared alongside the first. With a mighty growl and flap of its wings, a humongous gargoyle lunged out of the hole. It hovered in the air, staring down at the two warriors.

They quickly realized that this must be the Fajarah leader, as it was at least five times larger than the rest, making it about three tree lengths tall. Marcellinus and Aloisia saw a shocking sight: the massive gargoyle held the two children in its titanic feet. The titan then tossed the children to two nearby smaller gargoyles as it slammed down to the ground with a thunderous roar. Marcellinus and Aloisia were knocked to the ground but quickly regained their balance. The beast slowly crawled towards them like a massive ape as it lunged its claws at the two warriors. Marcellinus and Aloisia rolled out of the way and rose to their feet, slashing the beast in the sides with their weapons. As blood poured from the wounds, the giant raised its head and let out a mighty roar, signaling to the other gargoyles that it needed assistance. Then all but the two holding the children swooped down to attack Marcellinus and Aloisia, while the giant gargoyle continued its onslaught as well. The two warriors were now putting on an impressive show as they dodged every which way to avoid the titan's attacks, all the while dodging the attack of the smaller ones. When they had a chance, the two warriors either attacked the large beast with a slash, or sliced and killed a smaller one. In no time, there were only five smaller gargoyles left (not including the two holding children), and the large one. The giant gargoyle was now in extreme pain as its body was covered in a multitude of cuts. It began to back off as it signaled for the other five to attack Aloisia all at once. She was caught off guard, not expecting to fight all five at the same time. She quickly killed the first two with slashes of her spear, but the remaining three proved to be too fast as they slashed her across the arm with their mighty claws. Marcellinus saw her impending doom as he ran towards her, screaming, "Aloisia!" As he began to move near her, the massive gargoyle slammed its fist down, barring his path. It raised its other hand to attack Marcellinus. As it came slamming down, Marcellinus rolled out of the way. He hopped to his feet and took out his bow and arrows. He looked towards Aloisia, who was still in trouble. She was bleeding badly from her arm as she continued to dodge and block the three remaining gargoyles' attacks. Marcellinus knew he had to hurry, so as the massive beast went to slam its hand down once more to squash Marcellinus, he raised his bow and arrow and fired a shot, nailing the large gargoyle straight in its left eye. The giant howled in great pain as it placed its hands over the wound for comfort. Marcellinus had no time to waste as he shot another arrow at the three winged demons. The arrow struck the back of one, bringing it down to the ground in pain. He fired once more and struck another through the skull, killing it instantly. As the final one turned to see who killed its comrades, Aloisia lunged, putting her spear through the beast's heart, killing it. She removed her spear and approached the wounded gargoyle on the ground with the arrow still lodged in its back. She raised her spear high and slammed it into the beast's skull. Blood oozed from its wound and soaked up into the sand. At this moment, the massive Fajarah had finally recovered from its eye wound. The now cyclops gargoyle removed the arrow from its eye as it growled with a mighty roar. Marcellinus readied his sword as he and Aloisia approached the giant beast, but unfortunately, it rose to the skies once more. As it hovered there, blood continued to drip from its wounds to the ground below. It signaled for the last two small gargoyles holding the children to remain in front of it, thinking that Marcellinus and Aloisia would not attack if the children were in front. Marcellinus pulled out his bow and arrow in the hopes he would get a shot off, but he soon realized that it was very risky as the arrow might hit a child. The two children were both crying as they were forced to fly in circles.

The two smaller ones swooped down to attack the warriors using the children as shields. Marcellinus knew this to be a mistake as he tossed a knife to Aloisia, who nodded back; she knew what to do with it. Marcellinus readied his bow and arrow and aimed for the beast's skull, as it was still uncovered. When he was releasing his arrow, Marcellinus mumbled to himself, "Big mistake, beast." The arrow flew deep into the gargoyle's skull, killing it instantly, causing it to release the child from its arms and into the safety of Marcellinus's hands as the gargoyle came crashing down to the ground. Aloisia waited for her gargoyle to get closer, and as it took a swipe at her body, she leaped over its arm and plunged the knife deep within the side of its face. It dropped to the ground, dead, and it too released the child it was holding. Aloisia made a graceful leap to grab the falling child. Both children were now safe as the massive gargoyle screamed with anger. It then began to fly away, but with quick precision and agility, Aloisia grabbed her spear and threw it high into the air at the beast. It successfully struck the beast in the right wing, causing it to fall to the ground with a mighty smash. Marcellinus and Aloisia quickly approached the injured beast as it squirmed on the ground. It saw the two running towards it, so it began to kick and slash with its hands and feet. Marcellinus leaped over the first swipe and, with excellent mobility, brought his sword down with a mighty slash, cutting straight through the right arm of the beast. It screamed in incredible pain as blood gushed from the severed arm. Like lightning, the two warriors jumped on top of its chest, and they each plunged their weapons deep into the heart of the beast, killing it instantly. They removed their blood-stained weapons as the lifeless body of the gargantuan gargoyle began to sink into the sand. They climbed down and ran back to the children, who were now smiling and cheering. The children both clapped and hugged Marcellinus and Aloisia as they each said thank you.

The four of them made their way back to Kermanshah, to be greeted by the weeping parents of the children. The two children ran to their parents with open arms, as the mother and father smiled at Marcellinus and Aloisia, saying, "Thank you. Thank you so much, kind strangers. You shall not be forgotten for the great deed you have done today. You shall surely be blessed." Marcellinus and Aloisia smiled as the villagers came to greet them with smiles and pats on the back. One of the villagers also offered the two warriors a place to stay for the night and free bandages and herbs to heal their wounds. They heartily accepted the kind offer of the gentleman.

As nightfall quickly came, Marcellinus and Aloisia began walking to the house where they would be staying for the night. Marcellinus spoke to Aloisia. "Aloisia, do you need my help with your arm?"

She turned to Marcellinus and shook her head, saying, "No, it's okay. It's only a scratch. I can do it myself."

Marcellinus smiled in response, which quickly turned to sadness as he put his head down, facing the ground. He spoke. "You know, I thought I was going to lose you today. I got really scared,. I do not want anything bad to happen to you."

Aloisia smiled as she lifted Marcellinus's head with her hands and said, "Don't worry, Marcellinus. It will take a lot more than a little scratch to get rid of me."

Marcellinus looked into her big beautiful eyes as he smiled and said, "All right. Just…just be more careful from now on, Aloisia." She just smiled and giggled as the two made their way inside to rest for the evening.

The next morning, they were greeted by the children's parents and the children, who hugged them once again. The father spoke as he placed a sack on the ground. "We wanted to thank you for saving our children yesterday. All we have to give you is this sack of food and extra clothing."

Marcellinus spoke, "Oh, you do not have to give us anything. I fight to bring peace."

The man shook his head and smiled, saying, "No, it's fine. No trouble at all. We *want* you to have this, so please take it."

Marcellinus smiled as he picked up the sack, saying, "Thank you very much." After showing Aloisia the sack, the two made their way out of the village and continued their long quest once more.

# Chapter 16

About a two day journey delivered the two to a whole new country, the country of Iraq. This country was covered from head to toe with seemingly endless desert. The two slowly but steadily made their way out of the dreadful desert heat to the next village on the map, Baghdad. The village was much larger than the previous villages. The buildings were all made of stone and they stretched for miles. The people looked relatively the same; however, the only difference was that many men wore small cup-shaped fezzes above their heads. The women wore silky see-through straps in front of their faces. The rest of their clothing was identical to the previous villages. Marcellinus looked at Aloisia and spoke. "This village is massive." Aloisia nodded, agreeing. They both began their long journey to the village's exit. Then they passed many colorful shops selling all kinds of objects, from fish to melons. Jewelry and clothing, all kinds of fruit, and many different kinds of meat lined the stores. As they walked past, Marcellinus heard the merchants speaking to him while waving their merchandise in the air. He at once recognized the language as Arabic. Shaking his head at each one's offer, Marcellinus and Aloisia continued their walk.

When they entered the center of the village, they felt the ground rumble. It started off softly and then quickly got harder and harder. Marcellinus looked at Aloisia with worried eyes, as people began running around in a hurry, and said, "What is happening? Is the village sinking?" Aloisia shrugged her shoulders as she had no idea. People started screaming as the rumbling came closer and got louder.

Marcellinus, clueless, grabbed a man running by and asked him what was going on. The man kept pulling away from the grip of Marcellinus's hand. Marcellinus brought him close to his face and asked him once more what was going on. The man got nervous but came to his senses and spoke, "The beasts are attacking the city! The No Yaw Ah Doe Nuh Doe! The sand spirits! They have never entered the city before! We are all doomed! Please, let me go!" Marcellinus released the man as he ran off screaming for cover.

Marcellinus spoke to Aloisia. "Aloisia, prepare your spear, for I believe trouble approaches." Just as she readied her spear and Marcellinus unsheathed his sword, the most enormous beast they had seen thus far emerged from the depths of the sand.

It stood a colossal ten tree lengths tall as it lunged forward with an deafening roar. The beast was truly foul as it stared down at the ant-like people below. The entire body was colored tan and had hard, leather-like skin. Only half of its body was seen above the sand, making this beast much larger than it appeared. The beast had four thin, tiny arms attached to its man-like chest. The arms could not have been more than two tree lengths long. The face was appalling, with a lion-like nose and three long, sharp fangs inside its mouth. The fangs seemed to be its only teeth, and they were positioned very strangely. Two were on the upper-right and upper-left of its mouth, while the last was directly in the middle on the bottom, facing upwards. Its eyes rested beneath its bald head, and they were a dark brown color. The creature raised its tiny human-like hands and began to smash every nearby buildings it could see. Marcellinus knew that the village would be destroyed in no time at this rate, so he and Aloisia had to act fast. As people ran or got crushed by falling building debris, Marcellinus and Aloisia approached the colossal beast's lower body in the sand, which was its chest. Marcellinus screamed at Aloisia to attack. They began to cut and slice the beast with extreme ferocity, only to find that the wounds were not damaging the creature enough. Blood was pouring out of the wounds, but the beast just seemed to ignore it. Marcellinus knew that this would not kill the beast fast enough, for the city would be destroyed before the creature fell. He turned to Aloisia and spoke. "Aloisia, we must scale the beast and strike at the head. This is the only way to destroy it quickly enough." Aloisia nodded, agreeing with Marcellinus. He gave her six of his knives and then grabbed her shoulder, saying, "Good luck." Then the two slowly began to scale the beast using two knives as makeshift ladders. They would stab the beast and use the knife to pull on and climb higher. Then they would use the next knife exactly the same way and continue up. The knives didn't seem to affect the beast at all as they continued stabbing and climbing. The journey was rough, for the beast kept moving rapidly. Eventually, they both reached the head of the beast. The creature finally noticed the two warriors as they climbed its face. It could not reach its head with its scrawny arms to pull them off, so it began to shake its head wildly to try and fling them off. Marcellinus and Aloisia held on as tight as they could, until the beast paused from the shaking to recover; then they continued higher and higher. The beast grew angrier and angrier as they were stabbing it in the face to climb it. They soon reached the top of the creature's skull after the third time it shook its head. As they stood on top, the beast had finally had enough. It slowly started to bend forward to face the sand once more. Marcellinus knew that it was going to return to the sand below, so he quickly looked at Aloisia and said, "Quick! We must penetrate its skull before it buries itself in the sand!" With great ferocity, they plunged their sword and spear deep into the skull of the beast. The creature returned to his upright position and howled with a mighty scream as blood poured from its skull. Marcellinus and Aloisia removed their weapons and began repeatedly striking the titan in the skull. After the seventh strike, the beast had finally had enough and screamed in sheer agony slowly and then fell to the ground, dead. When it fell, Marcellinus and Aloisia held onto the beast's head, using their knives as handles. They released the knives, however, as it neared the ground, and made a mighty leap to the ground below. The beast was indeed dead, but it caused considerable amount of damage as it landed on top of several buildings and some people, squashing them.

Just when Marcellinus and Aloisia thought it was all over, the rumbling returned as two more No Yaw Ah Doe Nuh Does appeared from beneath the sand. The two beasts looked at the dead one and angrily screamed in the sky. They too began smashing everything in sight. Marcellinus looked at Aloisia and said, "Aloisia, you know what we have to do. You must get the one over there on the right; I shall take the one on the left. We must make haste before more people die." Aloisia nodded as she made her way to her beast. Aloisia reached her beast first, and using two more knives, began to scale the beast like she had the previous one. Marcellinus reached his beast and thought for a moment, *Perhaps if I scale the beast's back, it will not notice me like the first one did and I can kill it by surprise.* So Marcellinus lunged on the creature's back, stabbing his knives deep into the back of the creature.

Meanwhile, Aloisia was nearing the creature's face as she too thought to herself, *Maybe I should go around the beast's head so it won't notice me.* So, like Marcellinus, Aloisia went around the head of the beast. Marcellinus was just reaching the back of his creature's head as Aloisia reached the top of hers. She immediately stabbed the beast in its skull, causing it to shriek in pain. The sand spirit Marcellinus was riding noticed the other screaming in pain. It hastily made its way over to Aloisia's beast. Marcellinus clung on for dear life as the quick movement of his beast cause him to nearly fall. As they approached Aloisia's beast, it was already too late for it, as Aloisia had struck a fatal blow, causing the beast to collapse, dead, to the floor. Marcellinus managed to reach the top of the skull to see the beast crash to the ground and watch as Aloisia leaped to safety. Marcellinus covered his ears as the beast let out a mighty roar. Marcellinus knew he had to act fast, for the beast was getting terribly upset and destroying many things in its path. Surprisingly, it began to look down as it got closer to the sand. Marcellinus knew it was trying to retreat to the ground, so he had to kill it quickly. He had no time to stab the beast in the skull, so he very quickly used his sword to carve a large circle in the beast's head, causing the piece of skin to fall to the ground, splashing blood everywhere. The beast was incredibly close to the sand now, as it knew Marcellinus was on its head. The beast's brain was revealed inside the hole Marcellinus had cut. With a swift strike, Marcellinus cut through the brain, causing the titan to roar in pain as it stood straight up once more. Marcellinus delved his sword deep into the recesses of the brain, causing the beast to subside its screaming as it came thundering down to the ground. Marcellinus leaped to safety as he watched blood pour out of the skull of his victim.

He wondered if it was finally over. People began to cheer and approach Marcellinus and Aloisia as she ran back to reunite with Marcellinus. An old man approached the two, claiming to be the ruler of the village. He looked at Marcellinus and Aloisia as he limped towards them and spoke. "Thank you so very much, kind strangers! You have saved my people." He smiled at the two warriors as his long beard waved in the desert wind.

Marcellinus looked at him and said, "You are welcome, old man. Tell me, what did those beasts want?"

The old man smiled and said, "Please call me Hussein. The No Yaw Ah Doe Nuh Does were three evil spirits of the desert. They have lived there for many generations, even before this village was built. Not long ago, my ancestors were confronted with the sand spirits who threatened to destroy Baghdad unless we offered them a sacrifice every month. My ancestors tried to plead with the No Yaw Ah Doe Nuh Doe, but they grew angry. It was either a sacrifice or the destruction of our village. So having no choice, we have sacrificed one person every month to the terrible beasts, in order to soothe their rage. This month, I had no one to sacrifice, for the person we were to sacrifice escaped. So thinking we broke our deal, the three creatures went on a rampage in our village. But now thanks to you two, we can finally live in peace once more!" Marcellinus smiled as they crowded around him and Aloisia, cheering.

Aloisia then asked Marcellinus, "What is going on? What did that old man say?" Marcellinus looked at Aloisia and told her everything. Then the two were asked to stay for the night, and the village held a grand feast in their honor.

The next morning, Marcellinus and Aloisia packed up their things as they made themselves ready to go to their next stop. Hussein and the villagers waved good-bye to the two warriors as they made their way out of town to their final destination point of the first half of their quest.

# Chapter 17

After several days travel, Marcellinus and Aloisia had found themselves in the country of Syria, Marcellinus's final stop before returning home. He and Aloisia stopped to gaze upon the many wonders of the country. It was lush, with green grass and many wild animals frolicking through the fields. There were many buildings scattered across the countryside made of stone.

After not long at all, they at last reached the port city of Dimashq. Never before had Marcellinus and Aloisia seen an actual city. Everyone seemed really refined as they shrugged their noses at Marcellinus and Aloisia for how they were dressed. The women and men looked like the people from Iraq and Iran, except they dressed in much fancier and colorful clothes. And the women did not hide their faces. They were instead adorned with gold, a nose piercing. Besides the Arabian-speaking tan people, there were many paler and more-refined-looking women and men walking around as well. The paler men and women were dressed rather funny, as the women sported long robes of many colors, but typically white, with their hair pinned up. The older men wore long white robes as well, but others also wore a shaggy shirt and shorts of different colors. Marcellinus realized that these people looked like him. Could this be where he had originally come from? He had always known he was different and couldn't possibly be Hototo's biological son. Hototo would never speak of it when Marcellinus would ask why he looked different. Although Marcellinus was curious, he knew he belonged in China with his father, Hototo. Aloisia looked at the pale people, too, and then looked at Marcellinus and spoke. "Marcellinus. Is this where you are from?"

Marcellinus looked at Aloisia and said, "No. I was born and raised in China. No skin color could ever change that fact."

Aloisia just smiled and said, "Oh. Okay." Marcellinus frowned, for he knew he was raised in China, but he couldn't have possibly been born there.

The two made their way across the city and soon reached some wooden docks overlooking the sea. The two stopped and stared in amazement, for they had never seen the sea before. It was truly a beautiful sight to behold as they watched the crystal blue waves crash upon each other over and over, creating small ripples in the water. The two made their way closer to the sea as a group of fishermen, dressed like the pale men, approached them. The leader spoke. "I wouldn't get too close to the water if I were you." The leader was a short man with a tubby beard and round belly; he was also bald. Marcellinus tried to recognize the language of the pale group of men. In a few seconds, he realized they were speaking Latin. Marcellinus asked the man to repeat himself. The man said, "I said I wouldn't get too close to the water if I were you. What's the matter, hard of hearing or are you just dumb?"

Marcellinus smiled, trying to hide his anger as he said, "I am sorry I did not hear you the first time. Why should we avoid the water?"

The group of men laughed as they couldn't believe what they had heard, for everyone in Dimashq knew why. Then as the laughter stopped, the same man spoke. "What do you mean, why? Because of the Kraken, of course!" Marcellinus and Aloisia looked puzzled. The man saw this and continued, "You two aren't from around here, are you? Well then, allow me to educate you on the Kraken. First of all, do you notice how there are no ships parked at this dock?" Marcellinus and Aloisia turned and looked around to see that the man's words were true. The man continued, "There are no boats here because the Kraken will destroy them like it has been doing for nearly a year now. You see, we used to sail our ships across this water to trade our goods with Italy and Greece. Since the Kraken showed up and started destroying our boats, we haven't been able to sell a thing, and many of us have resorted to becoming fishermen, fishing by the dock just to make a living."

Marcellinus then said, "Tell me of this Kraken."

The man continued, "The Kraken is an enormous monster that lives beneath the sea. Nobody has truly seen the Kraken's body, for when it is spotted by a ship, all that can be seen are its enormous tentacles. Using its tentacles it would smash the ship, sinking it to the bottom, killing the crew."

Marcellinus pondered for a moment. He thought that if he could destroy the Kraken, then the emperor could also trade his silk to Italy and Greece by ship. Marcellinus asked, "If the Kraken were destroyed, would the trading by ship commence?"

The man said with a laugh, "Of course! Don't get your hopes up though, for nothing can destroy the Kraken!"

Marcellinus unsheathed his sword as he spoke, "I am Marcellinus, and I am a warrior hailing from China. I have destroyed many beasts on my journey, and I am sure I can defeat this Kraken as well!"

The group of men busted out laughing as if Marcellinus had told a funny joke. After they wiped the tears of laughter from their faces, they saw that Marcellinus was quite upset as he stood there frowning. The man spoke once more. "You're serious?"

Marcellinus nodded his head as he said, "Yes, I am."

The group of fishermen looked at each other with great amazement, as they thought Marcellinus was crazy. Then the leader spoke once more. "Okay. If you want to die that badly, you can take the small boat I have over here." The group walked to the left into a small cabin on the docks as they continued to laugh. Once there, the man walked inside and pushed a small boat, just big enough for two, outside into the water. He spoke, "Here you go! You can paddle your way out there to your death!" He began laughing some more as he and the group walked away. Just before they walked away, the man paused his laughter to say, "What a fool!" and they continued out of the docks. Marcellinus looked at Aloisia as he explained everything to her and why they were standing by a boat. Aloisia was a bit worried, as she didn't favor water battles too much, remembering the fight against Kun.

Marcellinus put his hand on her shoulder and spoke. "Do not worry, Aloisia. You and I can do this together. But I will need your help. We have defeated many monsters together, and we shall continue to do so here." Aloisia smiled as she grabbed Marcellinus's hand softly.

They then made their way into the small boat. As they paddled, they noticed how peaceful it was out in the ocean. The only sound to be heard was the sound of waves splashing in the sea. It was very relaxing. They paddled pretty far out in the ocean and still found no sign of the mighty Kraken beast. Just as they were about to give up, they saw large bubbles appearing from under the water.

Suddenly, a titanic tentacle appeared before them. The tentacle was completely white, with suction cups that were a slightly darker shade of white. The end of the tentacle was long and pointy and ended in a diamond-shaped hand, littered with three rows of suction cups, which obviously was the hand portion of the tentacle. The suction cups extended all the way down the arm on the front side. The part sticking out of the water was at least two tree lengths long. Suddenly, three more tentacles popped up from the water. Marcellinus and Aloisia quickly sliced them with their weapons as the tentacles neared their ship. They heard a growl of sorts, and the tentacles retreated under the water as blood poured from the wounds. Without warning, four more tentacles popped out of the water to attack. The two sliced and diced once more, causing them to retreat back in the water. A mighty growl was heard as another tentacle came forth out of the water, grabbing the boat from the underside and tossing it like a doll. Marcellinus and Aloisia were flung from the boat, and as they floated, they asked each other if they were all right. They both nodded as they swam underwater with weapons ready to confront their adversary.

They saw a mighty beast swim towards them. It was clear as day in the bright blue colored ocean. It was an enormous squid. They saw the tentacles were much larger at about six tree lengths long each. It had twelve tentacles in all. The head was quite massive, and it had two large, oval-shaped eyes on the side of its head. The head was about seven tree lengths tall as well, and the eyes were about two tree lengths tall. It was white from head to toe, and the eyes were as black as night. The head ended in a strange triangular point, almost in the shape of an arrowhead. Its mouth was located beneath its head, hidden by its tentacle arms. It had small, pointy teeth, perfect for gripping onto prey.

The beast swam towards the warriors as Marcellinus readied his sword, knowing that knives wouldn't cut it this time like they did with Kun. The beast grabbed Aloisia and Marcellinus with two of its large tentacles, squeezing their bodies. Marcellinus managed to free his hand, which held his blade, and began to swing it as fast as he could underwater. With three swings, he managed to cut the tentacle of the beast clean off. Aloisia, on the other hand, was stuck and could not get free. The beast growled in pain as blood filled the ocean and its tentacle sank to the bottom. It angrily grabbed Marcellinus with another tentacle. Marcellinus made quick work of this one, as well, which caused the beast to scream in pain once more as Marcellinus cut off the arm, filling the ocean with even more blood. Aloisia was still trapped as Marcellinus swam to her. The Kraken tried to grab Marcellinus with its nine other free tentacles but to no avail. Marcellinus swam under and over them, and as he reached the tentacle imprisoning Aloisia, he cut it off with three mighty blows from his sword. Aloisia was now gasping for air as Marcellinus helped her swim to the top. When they both resurfaced for air, they were only able to gather enough air for a few seconds as the beast dragged them under by their feet with two more of its tentacles. Aloisia and Marcellinus quickly cut the tentacles in two, leaving the Kraken screaming in pain as it lost two more arms, leaving it with only eight. The water was now a bright crimson color as it was colored with blood. The Kraken had had enough as it approached the two with mouth agape and sprayed a dark black ink into the water, making visibility low. Marcellinus and Aloisia could no longer see as they made their way to the surface. They managed to surface and recover some more air. Almost immediately, the Kraken itself surfaced, waving its eight remaining tentacles frantically. As it charged towards them, growling, Marcellinus readied his bow and arrows and shot one after another, hitting the beast in two of its tentacles, forcing them to drop back in the water to recover. And with a third arrow, he shot the beast in the dead center of its right eye. The Kraken was now screaming in an immeasurable amount of pain as it flopped back underwater. Marcellinus and Aloisia quickly followed as they watched the beast remove the arrow from its eye. As fast as they could, they swam close to the beast to attack. As they neared the beast, it turned, so its one remaining eye saw them approaching. The beast began to swim away, but it was already too late, for Marcellinus and Aloisia struck with their weapons. Marcellinus missed the beast's other eye as it swam up, but hit the beast in the side. Aloisia expected this to happen and she swam higher up from Marcellinus and lunged her weapon forward. Her spear penetrated the final eye remaining as the Kraken hastily swam away from Marcellinus. She removed her spear as blood poured from the wound. The beast was now blind. As it twisted and turned in pain in the water, the two warriors immediately began stabbing it over and over again on the head, in the hopes of killing it. It tried to grab Marcellinus and Aloisia with its remaining tentacles but could not find them since it was blind. Finally, after several stabs of their sword and spear, the mighty beast let out a final scream as blood poured from its many wounds, and it sank to the ocean floor, motionless and dead.

Marcellinus and Aloisia returned to the surface once more and returned to their boat. As they paddled, they noticed many sharks starting to swim around them; they had probably come to feed on the carcass of the Kraken. As they continued paddling, one of the beast's tentacle ends surfaced. It had been somewhat eaten by the sharks, but Marcellinus grabbed it with his sword as proof of their victory.

When they neared the docks, many people gathered around them in amazement and shock, as they could not believe the Kraken hadn't killed them. Marcellinus rose to his feet as he docked the boat. He saw the same group of fishermen in the crowd. He yelled at them while tossing the tentacle towards them, "The mighty beast, the Kraken, has been slain!" The group of people looked down at the tentacle and, with their mouths agape, looked back up at Marcellinus and began to cheer and holler with excitement.

The leader of the fishermen spoke to Marcellinus, "Wow! I can't believe you actually killed the Kraken! How can I ever repay you? I can finally start my trading business again!"

Marcellinus spoke. "Well there is one thing you can help me with. I am on a quest for the emperor of China to create a road of trade from the palace to here in Syria. So I need proof of my travel here. If you can help me find something to bring back to the emperor, I would be much obliged."

The fisherman spoke as he rubbed his chin, "Hmm…what could I give you that would convince your emperor of your travels here?" As he scratched his head, he raised his finger in the air and shouted, "I know! Come with me!" Marcellinus and Aloisia followed the man to his home within the city. He approached the door and turned around to speak to Marcellinus. "Wait here. I'll be right back." In a few minutes, the man returned with a small golden necklace with a picture of Alexander the Great on it. He handed it to Marcellinus as he spoke. "Here, take this. This necklace belonged to my great-grandfather. He was a general in Alexander the Great's army. He received it for doing some great deed or something; I'm not really sure. It was passed down to me, but I have no son to pass it down to myself. And I don't really have any use for it myself, so you can have it. The emperor will definitely believe you once he sees this!"

Marcellinus was very pleased and shocked to receive such a valuable gift. He spoke to the man, "Thank you very much, sir. I shall not forget your generosity."

The man laughed as he spoke to Marcellinus, "Generosity? Ha! You crack me up, Marcellinus. It's the least I could do for you. After all, you destroyed that foul beast, the Kraken. You were able to give me my job back!"

Marcellinus smiled and said, "All right. Well I must be heading back home to China now. Thank you again."

The man then smiled as he spoke, "Sure, no problem. And if you are ever in Syria again, be sure to visit! We can swap tales of our journeys over dinner."

Marcellinus waved as he walked away and said, "I will! Good-bye!" He placed the necklace within his sack. Then Marcellinus and Aloisia exited the city, preparing to make their long journey back home.

# Chapter 18

Marcellinus and Aloisia traveled back through many of the villages that they had previously been to before. As they passed through each one, they stopped for a moment to say hello to the people they had saved, and then continued on their way.

After fifteen days and nights, the two had reached the village of Mashhad once again. Marcellinus looked at the map. The path the map showed revealed a shortcut back to China, to the south. Marcellinus and Aloisia decided to head in that direction. After three days and nights, they found themselves back in Turkmenistan and in a new village named Kalai Mor.

The village was much different than any they had previously seen. It was nestled in the middle of a jungle. The people there looked the same as the others in Turkmenistan, but they bore no beards or hats on their heads. They instead wore small cloth-like diapers around their waists as their only clothing, while carrying crude spears as weapons. The women wore plain cloth dresses over their bodies. These native people lived in wooden houses built high in the trees and along the ground. They had no shops like the previous villages.

Nervously, the two warriors hastily made their way out of the village, as the natives looked as though they wanted to harm Marcellinus and Aloisia. Just as they neared the exit, one man approached them, speaking Turkmen. "Be wary of the Ya-te-veo."

Marcellinus looked at the man, puzzled, and spoke. "Ya-te-veo?"

The man nodded as he continued, "The Ya-te-veo is the god of this jungle. It doesn't like strangers. If you continue, you will surely be killed."

Marcellinus frowned as he shrugged by the man, saying, "I will take my chances." The man looked at the two as they traveled from the village, into the distance.

As the two made their way through the jungle, they heard many birds singing and bugs chirping. They hacked and slashed their way through the overgrown terrain until they came to an open field. As they stopped to rest, they noticed all the birds and insects had stopped making noises. Marcellinus and Aloisia looked up at the trees, puzzled by this fact. Suddenly, without warning, four large vines sprang forth from the ground with a crack.

The vines each stood about seven feet tall and were green all the way down their bodies. Attached at the top were small purple flower buds, which opened suddenly, revealing a four-way split mouth attached to it. The mouth was split open in the shape of an X. Each end was equipped with small, buzz-saw-like teeth. A small, thin tongue stretched forth from the middle as it spat drool upon the ground. Each one gave out a tiny shriek as it waved around in a somewhat dancing manner.

Then, one by one, the small vines began to strike at Marcellinus and Aloisia. Although tall, the vines were not very thick, so the two warriors were able to cut through them like paper. As each one fell to the ground, what looked like green blood oozed from the open wounds and the vine scurried back under the ground. The two continued to block and strike, and soon the four vines were killed. Immediately afterward, the ground began to shake quite tremendously.

Soon a massive vine sprang forth from the ground and stretched high in the air. When it stopped, it stood an impressive twelve feet tall. The vine's body was green as well, but this particular vine body was different as it was adorned with massive thorns that stuck out a good five inches each. The four giant, dark green leaves at the tip of the vine spread open to reveal a beautiful bright yellow flower bud. The beauty of the bud disappeared though as it opened up to reveal a hideous mouth. The mouth was in an X shape like the smaller purple ones. Its teeth were buzz-saw-like as well, just longer at about three inches each. As drool fell to the ground, three long and thick slimy tongues poured out from the mouth of the beast. The tongues were quite long, stretching about eight feet.

Marcellinus and Aloisia readied their sword and spear as the battle began. The Ya-te-veo made about twenty more smaller vines come forth from the ground to attack the two warriors. Marcellinus and Aloisia began blocking attack after attack as they hacked and slashed through the onslaught of vines. Green blood littered the floor, and soon, the vines were no more. Outraged, the mutant plant screeched as about forty more vines appeared from beneath the ground. The onslaught continued as Marcellinus and Aloisia proceeded to block and decapitate the many vines ahead of them. Soon, all the smaller vines had fallen, but Marcellinus and Aloisia grew weary. Marcellinus and Aloisia looked at each other as Marcellinus spoke. "Aloisia, we cannot keep this up for much longer. We must kill the large one and perhaps the smaller ones will stop appearing." Aloisia nodded as the two charged for the large bud. As they neared it, forty more smaller vines sprang forth. Marcellinus and Aloisia quickly hacked through the vines they encountered in front of them and finally reached the giant bud. The smaller ones continued to attack as the giant bud stretched forth its long tongues to grab a hold of the two warriors. With a mighty swing, Marcellinus cut through the tongue stretching towards him, causing a waterfall of blood to spray forth from the wound. The tongue hastily retreated inside the mouth of the beast. However, two tongues still remained, and as Aloisia was attacking the smaller vines, one of the tongues managed to grab her around the leg. She was lifted into the air, hovering upside-down over the beast's mouth. She knew if she cut the tongue now she would surely fall inside the beast's mouth. Marcellinus knew he had to act quickly, so ignoring the smaller vines, he quickly slashed the giant bud in the side of its vine-like body. Green blood poured out as the beast looked down at Marcellinus and screamed in pain. The massive bud dropped Aloisia on the ground, and she quickly sprang to her feet to begin attacking the smaller vines surrounding her. Marcellinus leaped back as the massive bud ceased screaming and lunged towards him, snapping its mighty jaws, trying to bite Marcellinus. Marcellinus yelled at Aloisia, "Aloisia! Take care of the smaller vines around me and I will kill the large one!" Aloisia nodded as she ran behind Marcellinus. She covered Marcellinus well as she sliced through each small vine, one by one. The large beast was now in a face-off with Marcellinus. It lunged, directing the two tongues at Marcellinus, who quickly slashed through both tongues instantly, causing blood to flow from the wounds. The tongues retreated into the bud's mouth. It let out a fierce roar as it began to lunge at Marcellinus, snapping its mighty jaws. Marcellinus rolled to the left and right of the gaping maw and quickly rose to his feet to give the beast a fierce slice. Blood littered the ground now and made a small green lake of sorts. After many rolls and dives to the left and right, and many slashes, Marcellinus swung his sword, delivering a mighty fatal blow to the massive flower bud. As the large decapitated head flew to the ground, it let out a final terrifying screech. Blood sprayed out of the decapitated massive vine as it wiggled and squirmed as if it were dancing in the air. Soon it crashed to the ground, remaining motionless. As the large bud died, all the smaller ones fell to the ground dead as well.

The two warriors wiped the sweat from their brows as they approached each other, each asking the other if they were all right. After checking on each other, the two warriors continued to hack and slash their way out of the jungle as the birds and insects resumed their melodious songs. Soon they found themselves out of the jungle and facing grassy plains, and they ran towards their next stop.

# Chapter 19

The two warriors found themselves in another new country, the country of Afghanistan. After another six days and nights of travel over hills and mountaintops, Marcellinus and Aloisia arrived at a village named Kabul. The village and its inhabitants were quite similar to the people of Iran and Iraq. The village seemed peaceful as Marcellinus and Aloisia walked by the smiling faces of the people. Marcellinus and Aloisia seemed at peace, for they could possibly leave a village without having to fight a monster. As they stocked up on food and supplies at the nearby merchants, Marcellinus and Aloisia looked up at the sky and noticed it growing very dark, as thunderous clouds appeared over the sun, eclipsing it. Marcellinus spoke to Aloisia. "Is it going to rain?" Suddenly, without warning, a large black hole appeared in the ground directly in front of the two warriors, extending in size. It was at least fifteen feet wide as Marcellinus and Aloisia drew their weapons. He looked at Aloisia and said, "What kind of sorcery is this?" A large black beast emerged from the hole, leaping high into the air and smashing down to the ground. The hole quickly closed up afterwards, and as people noticed the beast, they began to run and hide inside their homes, screaming. Marcellinus and Aloisia stared at the gigantic beast before them in awe as they prepared to defend themselves.

The beast was massive indeed. It was black from head to toe and covered in long, thick black hairs, making the beast quite furry. Amazingly, it had three heads, one on the left, on the right, and in the middle. And each was equipped with two ears, two eyes, a mouth, and nose. The beast was vaguely in the shape of a large canine, and it stood there, growling at the two warriors. Each one of its six eyes glowed a demonic crimson red. The ears were all long and pointy, at about five inches long each. Each head had a large, gaping maw full of three-inch razor sharp teeth. As each head opened its mouth, it revealed a long, slobbery tongue extending forth. As it growled, saliva dripped from its mouths, splashing onto the ground. The titanic dog stood tall at about two tree lengths tall. It had four beefy legs with five sharp claws attached to each toe. Although quite beefy and muscular, it was exceedingly skinny as the entire skeletal structure showed through its skin, as if it were starving to death. The most noticeable bones were its ribs and three spinal columns connecting to the back. The tail was long and even furrier than its body, as the hair frizzled out in tiny spike-like appendages. The tail was about seven feet long.

Then, to Marcellinus and Aloisia's surprise, the demonic beast began to speak in Chinese. "Master…sent… Mogui…to…kill…Marcellinus." It growled with rage, as drool continued to drip from its gaping maws. Marcellinus and Aloisia were still shocked to hear the beast speak as it lunged towards them to strike. They rolled to the left and right, barely dodging the beast's left and right heads. It quickly turned around and began a second charge as it growled. It stopped and began to lunge at Marcellinus. Marcellinus did his best to block the oncoming strikes from the beast's three heads. The beast was incredibly quick, however, making this a difficult task for Marcellinus. Aloisia charged at the beast to try and stab it, but the beast noticed her coming with its left head and flung its leg back. It made contact with Aloisia, knocking her to the ground. She stumbled to her feet, the wind knocked out of her. Realizing she had no other choice, she threw her spear at the titanic dog, jabbing it in its side. The beast threw its heads back as it let out a mighty howl in pain. Marcellinus quickly made his way to Aloisia and tried to catch his breath.

Marcellinus spoke to Aloisia as the beast scrambled to release the spear from its side. "Thank you. I thought I was dead for sure."

She nodded as she said very seriously, "Of course." Marcellinus, having caught his breath, readied his bow and arrows and began to shoot the beast from afar. One by one, the arrows pierced the beast's hide as blood poured out of each wound. However, the large canine was able to remove the spear from its side at long last. Blood dripped down from the gaping wound. There were about eight arrows lodged into its side as it growled with incredible ferocity. It turned to face Marcellinus once more as Marcellinus re-equipped his sword. The beast made another charging dash at Marcellinus, to begin another onslaught, as Aloisia ran to recover her spear. She noticed the beast only seemed interested in attacking Marcellinus for some reason. She tried to approach the beast again, and this time, she successfully snuck behind its back, slicing it near its back left leg. It howled in pain once more and turned to face Aloisia. The beast seemed irritated now as it began striking her with gaping maws. Marcellinus saw this as his chance. He leaped onto the beast's back and, grabbing chunks of its thick fur with his hand, began to stab the beast in the back with his other hand. The mighty canine was howling in pain as it dropped down to the ground and began to roll. Marcellinus was only able to get three stabs in. He noticed the beast rolling along the ground so, to avoid being squished, Marcellinus leaped off its back just in time. The beast was now limping in pain as blood littered the ground where it stood.

The three of them stood there staring at each other for a while before the beast finally ran towards them to attack once more. It attacked Marcellinus and Aloisia and the same time with its three heads. Marcellinus and Aloisia blocked the attacks as fast as they could, and then Marcellinus screamed at Aloisia, "Go for the heads! Kill the heads and the beast will surely die!" Aloisia heard this and began to counter attack. After blocking several attacks, Marcellinus had a clear shot for the right head he was battling. With a mighty lunge, he stabbed his sword deep into the skull of the beast's right head. A quick and loud whimper was heard as the head flopped down, motionless. Blood poured out of the wound as Marcellinus removed his sword. The middle head began to attack Marcellinus now, while Aloisia continued her attack on the left head. Finally, the left head was clear for an attack. Aloisia sliced its neck, making blood pour from the wound. As it reared back to howl in pain, she gave the head another mighty slash, this time cutting through it entirely. The decapitated head flew through the air and landed behind the beast as blood oozed out of the neck wound. Aloisia joined Marcellinus in attacking the middle and final head. The colossal canine now seemed worried as it slowly backed away while continuing to lunge its head to try and bite Marcellinus and Aloisia. With two mighty lunges, the two warriors managed to jam their weapons deep into the beast's head at the same time. As they removed their weapons, the giant canine let out a mighty roar and blood poured from its remaining skull. With a thunderous roar, the beast crashed to the ground, now deceased. Marcellinus and Aloisia looked on in amazement as the beast's body was magically engulfed in flames, including the decapitated head, and turned into black ashes. The ashes then blew away into the air as the clouds dissipated from in front of the sun, revealing a bright, beautiful day once more. It was almost as if the battle never took place.

The people then emerged from their homes and began to cheer and clap their hands. Marcellinus and Aloisia had saved their village. One man spoke in a strange dialect that Marcellinus recognized as a form of the Persian language called Dari. "Thank you, kind strangers. Our village has been saved from that demon."

Marcellinus then smiled as he said, "You are welcome. It was no trouble at all."

The man continued, "Please allow me to give you a room for the night." He led Marcellinus and Aloisia to a nearby inn so they could rest for the night.

Before going to sleep, Marcellinus entered Aloisia's room to speak with her. "Aloisia. I wanted to ask you something."

Aloisia smiled as she asked, "What?"

Marcellinus then continued, "Do you think it was strange that the beast we killed today could speak our language?"

Aloisia looked concerned as she spoke. "Yes, it was strange at first. But I think I know why." Marcellinus looked quite puzzled as she continued, "I recognized that beast from my grandfather's book. I remember it saying that as he traveled through the mountains to the north of China, he encountered a similar beast dragging victims into the hole that it appeared from, like we saw today. I also remember it saying that the beast could speak small words of our language. My grandfather then continued to say that as the beast pulled humans into the hole, that the beast was ordering smaller demons to grab the younger humans. So this beast must be a higher ranking demon in the underworld. I remember my grandfather giving it a peculiar name in his journal. He called it cerberus."

Marcellinus looked troubled as he said, "But why would the demons want to kill me? Perhaps as revenge for the monsters we have slain?" Aloisia looked saddened as she did not know the answer. Marcellinus continued, "We'd best be on our guard until we reach home, just in case more demons appear." Aloisia nodded, agreeing with Marcellinus. The two said good night to each other, and Marcellinus returned to his room. They both went to bed for the night.

# Chapter 20

Marcellinus and Aloisia left the next morning, and after ten days and nights, the two finally found themselves back in their home country of China. Marcellinus took a deep breath as he said, "Finally, I am back in China. I am coming, Father. Please hold on."

Aloisia looked at Marcellinus and laughed as she said, "Yeah, now I'll be able to understand what people are saying again." Marcellinus chuckled back, and the two continued their quest forward.

About another day and night's journey brought them to a new village in China. This village was called Kashgar, according to the map. As they entered the village, they both seemed satisfied with the sight of a Chinese village. They let out a sigh of relief once more. They felt completely at home. There were many stone houses along the way, and men and women wearing blue and red Shenyis and Qujus. Kashgar wasn't very big, though, as Marcellinus and Aloisia walked through it.

The people here seemed a little depressed or angry, so the two warriors tried to quickly make their way out. Suddenly, clouds began to form again, causing another eclipse of the sun, as thunder boomed in the background. Marcellinus and Aloisia looked on with worried faces, as they knew what was to come next: a demon. When the two prepared their weapons for battle, a loud voice echoed across the land. The voice was very deep and raspy as it spoke. "Fools! Marcellinus and Aloisia! You two shall pay with your lives for what you have done!" With a blinding flash of light, lightning struck the ground in front of the two warriors. From the explosion of light, a large demon beast emerged. The beast stood there, growling at the warriors. The voice boomed once more, "My servant Kemaila, the chimera, will obliterate the both of you! Destroy them, Kemaila!" The voice laughed and faded away along with the clouds.

The chimera that the voice had summoned was truly a daunting foe to behold. Just like the cerberus, it had multiple heads, only this one had four. It was as long as two trees and as tall as one and half. The body was split in two, as the front half was that of a lion, and the back, a goat. The front part of the body was covered in yellow fur and adorned with two mighty paws on its front two legs, equipped with razor sharp claws. The head in the middle of its body was that of a lion as well. It had a proud and mighty dark brown mane, with long, pointy cat ears. The face, nose, and mouth were copies of a lion's. The mouth opened up, revealing sharp teeth inside. Its whiskers were quite long, as well. The lion's eyes were a bright green color. The backside was covered in gray fur, and its back legs were black and hoofed like a goat's. The head on the left was an exact copy of a goat's as well. It was covered in black fur from head to toe and had a small goatee under its chin. The mouth was equipped with two-inch-long sharp teeth. Its two ears hung low and droopy at about six inches long. The head also had two long, pointy, and straight horns atop it, which were a yellowish color. The eyes of the goat were a bright blue instead of green. The right head of the beast was an exact copy of a mighty dragon's. The dragon's body was a pinkish color and covered from head to toe in scales. It had long, black, six-inch spikes all along its backside. The face was long and pointy as it opened its impressive maw, which stretched to about twelve inches. The mouth was riddled with razor sharp teeth. Atop the head were two long, sharp horns that were at least sixteen inches long each. The dragon's eyes glowed bright yellow. The back of the entire beast was equipped with two of the dragon's wings. The wings stretched to an impressive two tree lengths each. Like the head, the wings were also pink with scales. The middle of the wing ended with a sharp spike-like finger extending forth. Much like the wing of a bat, it had thin strips of skin stretching all the way down its wing, with black membranes separating each finger. Finally, the beast's tail was a head itself. It was a long and humongous snake. The snake-like tail hissed as it danced in the sky. The tail was at least two tree lengths long. Its body was green with dark green diamond-shaped patches along its entire back. The tail was also very scaly, as the bright crimson red eyes shined forth. The snake-like tail extended its long, forked tongue as its five-inch mouth opened, revealing two three-inch fangs.

The beast stood there, growling at the two warriors at first, as drool dripped down each head's mouth and slopped onto the ground. Then without a word, the demon lunged forward to attack Marcellinus and Aloisia. The lion and dragon heads began to bite at Marcellinus as he blocked their attacks, and the goat head began to strike Aloisia. The snake head stretched around and began to strike at Aloisia as well. After a few blocks with his sword, Marcellinus got a clear shot at the beast's two heads. Like lightning, he slashed the dragon and lion heads along the neck. The chimera leaped backwards as it screamed in pain. Blood dripped from the wounds as the dragon head reared back and shot forth a large trail of flame towards Marcellinus. Marcellinus leaped to the side and continued to run and leap until he jumped into the middle of two stone houses. The beast ran over to the small gap, and the dragon head began to breathe fire once more inside the hole, but Marcellinus had already made his way around to the other side of the house. Aloisia saw him coming, and to divert the attention of the snake head, she charged at it with her spear waving madly in the air. The snake saw her and the two clashed in battle.

The flames finally halted as Marcellinus ran up to the side of the beast to attack. In the last second, the dragon head turned to see Marcellinus coming and immediately breathed fire in Marcellinus's direction. Marcellinus rolled left and plunged his sword deep into the side of the beast as he rolled up to his feet. The beast was now very angry and began to attack Marcellinus with all three heads now. Marcellinus blocked bite after bite from the three terrible heads, while

Aloisia battled the snake head. Aloisia finally had an opportunity to attack the snake when it lunged to the right to strike. She quickly leaped to the left and chopped down her spear in the air like she was cutting wood. And with a fast and swift strike, the snake's head was cut off. The chimera screamed in pain as blood poured out of its open wound in the back. The snake's head began to squirm back and forth on the ground, screaming, as it finally died. The chimera then ceased its attack on Marcellinus as it leaped backwards. Then Aloisia rejoined Marcellinus as the beast spread its gigantic wings and took to the air. As it flew overhead, the beast spewed forth flames from the dragon head. Marcellinus and Aloisia quickly rolled to the right and left to avoid the flames. Then, the beast made a circle to turn around and try and burn its victims once more. Marcellinus readied his bow and arrows and shot forth an arrow, penetrating the beast's left wing. Stunned, the beast growled very loudly and breathed fire towards the ground. The two warriors continued dodging the onslaught, and Marcellinus readied more arrows. This time, as the beast returned, Marcellinus shot three arrows towards the same wing. They each penetrated the beast, and the chimera came smashing to the ground, leaving a small crater where it landed. It quickly hopped out of the hole and observed its wing, which was now useless as a large hole was ripped in the middle of the wing's membrane. It stretched out its wounded wing, causing the wing to rip even more, this time totally ripping the membrane in half. Now the wing flapped in the wind like dead skin. The chimera yelled with ferocity as it angrily charged towards Marcellinus and Aloisia. The dragon head started attacking Marcellinus with bites and small flame bursts, which Marcellinus had to block and roll out of the way of. The lion and goat heads began biting at Aloisia. After a few blocks with her spear, Aloisia saw an opening, and with great agility, plunged her spear deep into the head of the goat. The other two heads screamed in agony as she removed her spear. The goat head was gushing blood from its wound as it plopped down and hung there like a piece of dead meat. The lion head was enraged and began to attack Aloisia. The dragon head resumed attacking Marcellinus after screaming in pain for a mere half a second. Fire spewed forth from the mighty dragon's maw, but Marcellinus leaped to safety each time. Marcellinus had finally had enough, and as the dragon spewed forth more flame, he quickly stepped to the left of it and plunged his sword deep into the beast's neck, causing it to shriek in pain. He removed his sword and, with a mighty slash downwards with his sword, decapitated the dragon, causing blood to spray out of the wound. The dragon's head wriggled on the ground and finally lay motionless. As the lion head continued its attack on Aloisia, Marcellinus plunged his sword deep into the lion's neck, causing it to scream in pain and turn towards Marcellinus to attack. This allowed Aloisia to drive her spear deep into the beast's skull. The lion head let out a mighty growl as it stood on its hind legs and fell backwards on the ground with a loud smash, dead. Just like the cerberus, the chimera, including the decapitated heads, burst into flames and turned to ashes. The ashes blew away in the wind and all was peaceful once more.

The villagers emerged from their houses and began to cheer for Marcellinus and Aloisia for defeating the demon. They were once again invited to stay at an inn for the night.

While the two were at the inn, Marcellinus approached Aloisia in her room as she was preparing for the night's rest and asked, "Aloisia, why do you think the demons want to halt my quest? Why do they want to kill me?"

Aloisia looked at Marcellinus and said, "I don't know. It's very strange." Marcellinus continued, "Did your great-grandfather or grandfather's books speak of demons behaving like this?"

Aloisia pondered for a while and then looked up at Marcellinus and spoke. "No, I have never read anything like this in either book."

Marcellinus became very troubled as he spoke again. "I fear my time will soon come to an end, for the demons, it seems, will not rest until I am dead."

Aloisia approached Marcellinus, who was now sitting on her bed, and sat down next to him. She placed her hand on top of his hand and said, "Don't worry, Marcellinus. No matter what beast the demons throw at us, I will never leave your side in battle, or as a friend."

Marcellinus blushed as he looked down her soft hand, now caressing his hand, and said, "Thank you, Aloisia. You are truly a great friend." Marcellinus looked down as he got upset with himself. He clearly wanted to say they were more than just friends. What of Princess Nangong? How could he break his vow to the emperor's? He stood and said good night to Aloisia as he made his way to his room for the night.

# Chapter 21

The two warriors left the village in the morning. After two more days and nights of travel, they arrived at another new village, the village of Aksu. The village was rather large compared to the other villages in China. They walked past many markets and stone houses, and noticed the men working on every house. It seemed the entire town was remodeling. Marcellinus had seen this before and feared the worst as another beast might inhabit this land as well. Marcellinus approached one of the villagers repairing his house and asked, "Excuse me, but what has happened here? Why are all of you rebuilding?"

The man paused for a moment to speak with Marcellinus. "The terrible dragon, Shenlong, has attacked and destroyed our village. Many of our houses were badly burned or blackened in the mighty beast's flames." Marcellinus asked more about Shenlong. The man responded, "Shenlong is a mighty dragon who has reigned over this land for many years now, and some say he is god of the wind and rain. Every two weeks, he appears from the heavens and flies down to our village and quickly burns it down to the ground. He is so massive that nothing we do can ever stop him. We will all surely die. It has been about two weeks since the beast came last, so he is sure to make his appearance again today. You two must leave now while you can."

Marcellinus and Aloisia frowned as Marcellinus spoke. "No, we are traveling warriors and have fought many beasts. What Shenlong is doing here is appalling, so we shall stop him."

The man looked at Marcellinus and spoke once more. "How can you stop him? It is our curse to be plagued by this beast. You are just two people. You can never hope to win."

Marcellinus continued, "I am Marcellinus, son of Hototo, the greatest swordsman in all of China. I will kill this dragon or die trying!"

The man seemed uneasy as he realized he could not talk Marcellinus or Aloisia out of attacking Shenlong. The man spoke. "Fine. If you two want to die, then by all means, go ahead and try and kill Shenlong."

All of a sudden, a woman came running down the road, screaming, "Shenlong! Shenlong is coming!" The man and all the other villagers quickly ran inside to the safety of their homes as Marcellinus and Aloisia made their way to the center of the village. As they looked up into the sky, they saw a massive wingless dragon fly down towards them. Shenlong only grew larger and larger as it approached them. The dragon let out a mighty roar, and the two were able to get a good look at it. The dragon was wingless, and it stretched its serpentine body in the air. Shenlong was as long as about fifty trees—a truly remarkable beast, indeed. It was covered from head to toe in bright ruby red scales. The dragon's back was adorned with short, frizzy, spike-like hair that was a yellow sun color. Shenlong had four beefy legs, two in the middle and two near its back end. Each leg was equipped with four toes with razor sharp claws that were at least ten inches long each. Its tail extended out in a wavy, flame-shaped, paper fan motion, as the yellow hair reached out to make this design. The underbelly was like a snake's and was also as yellow as the sun, and was separated by stripes indicating body segments. Atop its titanic head, Shenlong had two long and pointy horns, which were about fifteen inches in length. The dragon's mouth opened, revealing small, razor sharp teeth all along its edges, and a big, thick, forked tongue. The mouth was outlined with yellow hair, and two long, thin yellow whiskers branched from its nose. The eyes were quite large and they shone with a black tone.

As the beast neared the ground, Marcellinus began firing his arrows in the hopes it would damage the beast, but to no avail. Four arrows dug deep into the dragon's hide, but it did not seem to affect the colossal beast as it dive-bombed downwards and released a mighty flame. Marcellinus and Aloisia ran as fast as they could to the left and right to avoid the fire. The flames stretched as wide as the village itself. The two warriors barely managed to escape the flames. They quickly rose to their feet to see a few people running like mad, as they had caught on fire. They would soon fall to the ground and die from the burns. The dragon flew high and turned around to face the village and continued its assault.

Marcellinus knew the only way to stop the dragon was to get on its body and attack it directly. He yelled at Aloisia, "Aloisia! Please lend me some rope from your sack!" Aloisia removed her rope that she bought at a market in Iran and gave it to Marcellinus. He took out four arrows and began to tell Aloisia of his plan. "If I can get a clear shot at the beast with these arrows, we can scale its body with this rope and attack it directly." Aloisia thought it was a pretty good idea as she watched Marcellinus bundle the four arrows together. Then, using one end of the rope, Marcellinus wrapped the rope around the bundle of arrows and tied them together with a tight knot. He wrapped the rest of the slack around his arm. When the dragon was nearing the village again, Marcellinus aimed high in the sky, towards the beast. The arrows flew with incredible accuracy and plunged deep into the side of the beast. The dragon still seemed unscathed as Marcellinus grabbed the other end of the rope very tightly and turned to Aloisia with hand extended, saying, "Aloisia, grab my hand, quickly!" Aloisia grabbed Marcellinus's hand as he said, "Hold on tight and do not let go!" With a sudden jerk, the two went flying into the air, towards the beast's body, as the flames spewed forth, down into the village behind them. Then, as quick as they could, they began crawling across the rope to reach the dragon's body, like two monkeys on a vine. They soon reached the body of the dragon as Marcellinus dug a knife deep into the beast's side for support. He turned to Aloisia, grabbed her hand, and helped her get onto the dragon's body as well. Still holding her, he handed her two of his knives for her to use. She dug one in with her other hand and then released Marcellinus's hand and dug the other blade in with that hand. Marcellinus grabbed another knife and dug it deep into the side of the beast as well. The two were now clinging onto the beast as it soared high in the clouds. They managed to make their way to the backside, where they could actually somewhat stand on their feet. They noticed that the behemoth of a dragon was heading towards the village again. It was quite relentless. They hurried as fast as they could to reach the head, running and using the knives for balance when needed. They soon reached the beast's head. It was now aware of their presence. Marcellinus moved to the right side, as Aloisia went to the left. It began to do barrel rolls in the sky above the village in the hopes of shaking them off. The two warriors dug their knives into its face to hold on for dear life. After about seven barrel rolls, Marcellinus and Aloisia were beginning to feel rather sick, but luckily, the dragon paused its circular movement for the time being as it flew high in the sky, straight up. The two used this golden opportunity to unsheathe their weapons, and with two mighty strikes, plunged the weapons deep into each eye of the beast, blinding it. It screamed in terrible pain as blood and puss oozed from its eye sockets. The beast began to fall from the sky as the wounds in its eyes seemed to be fatal. As it plunged to the ground, Marcellinus grabbed onto Aloisia by her waist, and just as the beast hit the ground, they leaped from the beast and rolled safely along the ground. As they jumped from the beast, they heard the sound of breaking bones; the beast had snapped its neck into pieces. If it wasn't dead before, it was surely dead now.

The remaining villagers exited their homes and ran towards the two warriors with arms waving and much cheering. They were screaming, "We are free!" and, "Shenlong has been slain!" Marcellinus and Aloisia felt proud as women and children hugged them and men patted their shoulders. They were then asked to stay for a great feast that night as well as offered two rooms to stay in for the night.

After the great feast, there was much dancing and beautiful music. Aloisia looked over at Marcellinus as he was sitting around a small campfire, telling his story of how he slew the dragon to the children of the village. Aloisia walked over to Marcellinus, after paying her respects to the dead, leaving her group of people, who were also mourning the dead. As she walked over to Marcellinus, she got extremely nervous, for she wanted to ask him to dance. She knew they neared the end of their journey, so this could be her final chance. She stopped to take a deep breath as she gained some inner courage and then tapped Marcellinus on the shoulder. Marcellinus turned to see who it was. He smiled at Aloisia, saying, "Yes? What is it, Aloisia?" Aloisia grabbed Marcellinus's hand and made him rise to his feet. She pulled him towards the group of dancing people. Marcellinus was feeling awkward as he asked Aloisia, "Aloisia, what are you doing? Where are we going?"

Aloisia turned to him with a smile and said, "I want you to dance with me, so come on!" Marcellinus blushed and got really nervous as the two made their way to the middle of the group of dancers.

Marcellinus stood in front of Aloisia, blushing, and said, "I…I do not really know how to dance. I have never done it before."

Aloisia smiled and laughed as she said, "Really? It's easy. I'll teach you. First put your hands here." Aloisia took Marcellinus's hands and placed them upon her hips.

Marcellinus was now blushing exceedingly as he said, "Are you sure this is how to do it?"

Aloisia said with a smile, "Of course. And then I put my hands here." Aloisia then reached around Marcellinus's neck and then rested her head on his bulky, naked chest. Marcellinus was now incredibly nervous as the warmth of Aloisia's body against his felt so good. Aloisia said, "Wow, your body is so warm. Like a soft coat of fur." She closed her eyes and gave Marcellinus a big hug as she said, "Mmm…" She could hear Marcellinus's heart beating really fast. She knew he was nervous and this made her giggle. She spoke. "Okay, now we move our feet like this. Slow, side-to-side steps as we move in a circle." They slowly began to dance, and Marcellinus did surprisingly well. The musician noticed the two warriors dancing, and he began to play a soft, romantic song on his flute. The two danced for a while and then Aloisia looked up at Marcellinus and said, "Wow, you're pretty good at dancing."

Then Marcellinus looked down at Aloisia. Their eyes made contact. Marcellinus saw her beautiful hazel eyes glowing in the moonlight as Aloisia stared into the loving eyes of Marcellinus. They leaned in for a kiss, but at the last moment, Marcellinus pulled away and said, "I am sorry, I just…cannot do this." He walked towards his room, leaving Aloisia standing alone by the roaring campfire with her hand on her mouth and a small tear beginning to develop. Then she ran to her room.

Marcellinus sat down on his bed and covered his face with his hands, and in frustration, he threw his sack of supplies across the room. He cupped his hands together as he began thinking. He wanted to kiss Aloisia, he really did. He was madly in love with her. What could he do? Should he remain loyal to the emperor or listen to his heart? Marcellinus knew not what to do. He remembered his father telling him when he was little, "A real man makes his own decisions, but a smart man follows the decisions of his heart. Remember this, my son: your heart will never lie." Marcellinus was now more confused than ever, for his heart wanted Aloisia, but he did not want to disobey the emperor's orders. He rolled over to try and get some sleep.

# Chapter 22

Marcellinus barely got any sleep that night and, as he awoke the next morning, he stumbled out of the bed, getting ready to prepare for his journey home. After grabbing everything he needed, he walked outside to see Aloisia waiting for him. They both gave each other uneasy glances as Aloisia spoke. "Good morning. Are you ready to go?"

Marcellinus nodded as he said, "Yes, let us go." They left the village while waving back to their newfound friends.

It would be three days and nights before the two would reach their next village. According to the map, this village was called Korla. As usual, it looked the same as all the other villages in China. While they were walking, they noticed a man and woman crying as they were packing up their belongings to move. Marcellinus and Aloisia approached the couple to see what was wrong. Marcellinus then spoke. "What is the matter? Why are you leaving the village?"

The man turned to Marcellinus and spoke as the woman continued to pack. "Oh. You must be new around here. My wife and I are leaving because we can no longer use the water from the lake to the East of here anymore." Marcellinus looked puzzled as the man continued, "We used to use the lake's water for everything, but since the beast inhabiting it showed up, no one can even get near the lake. Now all our crops have gone dry and died and our wells no longer sprout water. Many people have already left, so we are following in their footsteps."

Marcellinus frowned and spoke. "What beast do you speak of?"

The man looked down towards the ground as he said, "The great water serpent, Jormungandr. This leviathan has plagued our lake for five months now. It is too powerful for us to kill. We have tried many things. The only way to attack it would be to swim in the water with it, but that's suicide."

Marcellinus turned to Aloisia, and she nodded as if she were saying that she knew what had to be done. Marcellinus spoke to the man, "Please tell me of this lake. How far east is it? I will then face this Jormungandr and try to destroy it."

The man smiled and said, "Really? It is too powerful, though. You will surely die."

Marcellinus clenched his fists as he said, "I am Marcellinus. I was trained by Hototo Takeshi, the greatest swordsman in all of China. I have traveled far and faced many monsters and demons. And when I see those in need, I do my best to help them."

The man smiled as he said, "I truly respect your bravery, Marcellinus. Come with me; I shall take you to the lake myself."

Marcellinus smiled as he touched the man's shoulder and said, "Of course. Monsters and demons have no place in this world."

All three exited the village and traveled east for about a half a day's journey. And they all soon saw the lake a short distance away from where they were standing. The man stopped and pointed at the lake as he spoke. "There is the lake. Jormungandr is within, but this is as far as I go. I shall watch your battle from here." As Marcellinus and Aloisia made their way to the lake's edge, the man yelled out, "Good luck, brave ones! I shall be praying for your safe return!"

As Marcellinus and Aloisia approached the lake, they noticed the water was a beautiful, crystal clear blue. A rainbow assortment of flowers lined the edges of the lake. The lake itself was quite large and was about the size of a medium-sized village. They took deep a breath as they plunged into the water. The two immediately noticed how perfectly clear it was underwater. They did not swim for long when a massive serpentine beast came up from the depths of the lake and appeared right before their very eyes. As the massive serpent waved its long body back and forth, the two warriors got a very good look at it. The beast had to be as long as about thirty tree lengths. It was a musty gray color all over its body while looking quite slimy in appearance. The body was not quite as wide, however, as it was about only two tree lengths wide. In the back of the beast, it had two large and long arms protruding from each side. The arms were ten tree lengths long each. At the end of each arm was a lightly colored fin, about five tree lengths long. The fins shined with a bright yellowish-green tint. The front of the body had two short arms protruding from each side that it used as flippers. Each one was about three tree lengths long, with a bat-like appearance, just without the skin membranes, and ended in short spikes along the bottom. Moving up the head, they noticed seven small slits along each side of its body, indicating the gills. At the end of each slit was a small patch of skin flapping in the water with a pinkish tone to it. Nearing the head, they saw that the beast was adorned with two long horn-like arms on its sides. Each was an impressive seven tree lengths long, and equipped with eight tree lengths long fins that were also a yellowish-green tint. Its eyes were actually quite small and cylindrical as they glowed with an uneasy white glow. The beast's gaping maw opened to reveal massive twelve-inch-long teeth and a thick tongue. The mouth opened to easily reach a length of three tree lengths.

The beast growled, and the lake shook with the vibrations. Suddenly, it charged towards our warriors with lightning-fast accuracy. They both swam to the right and left, just barely missing being chomped, but the tail of the titanic serpent managed to whip Marcellinus across the body, temporarily making him dizzy. He quickly recovered to notice the beast returning to strike again. The beast approached Marcellinus when Aloisia was swimming to the beast's side. As it swam past, she plunged her spear into its body, causing the beast to growl and blood to leak from its wound. Marcellinus was relieved at this, for he would have not made it out of the way in time to avoid its bite. The beast made a quick circular motion to try and bite Aloisia when she was pulling her spear from its side. She then swam downwards just to have the serpent follow her. She quickly turned around and jammed her spear into the beast's open maw, causing it to force its mouth open. The beast was now wriggling and squirming in the water, splashing crazily as it could no longer close its mouth. Marcellinus approached the beast and plunged his sword deep into its hide. The beast snapped its mouth shut, causing Aloisia's spear to snap in two. Aloisia quickly swam to the bottom to recover the blade end of her spear as the leviathan swam towards Marcellinus to attack. Marcellinus saw the beast approach and readied his blade. The beast snapped its massive maw closed. Marcellinus quickly swam upwards, dodging its mouth, and quickly plunged his blade downwards, nailing the beast in its skull. Jormungandr was now wailing in pain as blood oozed forth from the wound. It splashed to the surface, continuing its screaming, Marcellinus took this time to catch his breath. Aloisia hastily followed close behind and surfaced, catching her breath as well. Then the beast shook its head rapidly as it flung Marcellinus onto the surface of the land nearby. Marcellinus slammed down on the ground and grabbed his side, which was now in severe pain. He managed to recover to his feet, watching the beast wriggle in the sky and come crashing down to the ground in front of him. Aloisia quickly swam to the shore and got out to run towards Marcellinus. The beast was still gasping for air, trying to slowly make its way back into the water, but Marcellinus, limping, approached the beast and quickly raised his sword high in the air to stab the beast. The leviathan then snapped its jaws at Marcellinus in an attempt to kill him. Marcellinus quickly leaped to the left and brought his sword down into the beast's eye, plunging it deep into the serpent's skull as far as he could make it go. With a final screeching scream, the leviathan was silenced as blood and eye puss rushed out of the wound once Marcellinus removed his sword. The beast was now deceased.

The man from the village came running towards Marcellinus as Aloisia joined them as well. The man stared at the dead body of the leviathan and spoke. "Wow! I can't believe you two managed to destroy Jormungandr!"

Aloisia looked at Marcellinus as he grabbed his side in pain and said, "Marcellinus, are you okay?"

Marcellinus, while still grabbing his side, spoke. "Yes, I will be fine. Nothing a few bandages and herbs will not cure." Aloisia and the man helped Marcellinus walk back to the village as nightfall approached. When they arrived, the man released Marcellinus into Aloisia's arms and ran through the village telling everyone of Marcellinus and Aloisia's efforts. Everyone rushed to Marcellinus and Aloisia, clapping and cheering and thanking them for a job well done. The people could now stay in Korla, for the lake was theirs again.

Marcellinus and Aloisia were offered rooms for the night and some herbs and bandages to help heal Marcellinus. Marcellinus made his way to his room with Aloisia's help and collapsed in his bed. Aloisia decided to heal him personally. He fell asleep quickly when she began to mix the herbs. She placed it on his wounds and massaged his sides for quite a while. Then, when everything seemed fine, she wrapped him up in bandages. As he slept, Aloisia looked upon his face and smiled. She leaned towards his ear and whispered, "Marcellinus, I love you." Aloisia stood up and made her way out of the room and into her bed, and slept soundly through the night.

# Chapter 23

The next morning, Marcellinus awoke feeling much better. He grabbed his sword, took a few swings, and smiled, delighted he could still fight just fine. The two warriors met outside, looked at one another, and smiled. Aloisia showed her broken spear to Marcellinus and said with a chuckle, "Well I guess I can no longer fight."

Marcellinus smiled and said, "Of course you can. Please hand me your spear." He made his way to a nearby house, which happened to be a smithy. Marcellinus asked the smithy if he could fix Aloisia's spear. Being very grateful that they had killed the leviathan, the man was more than happy to let Marcellinus use his smithy. After Marcellinus thanked the smithy, he pulled out a few of his knives and placed them in the fire. Within seconds, his knives melted in the fire, and he poured them into a long, cylindrical, metal frame. Then he began to meld a new handle for Aloisia's spear. Once finished, Marcellinus returned outside and gave Aloisia her rebuilt weapon. Aloisia smiled as Marcellinus said, "This handle is made of steel, so it will not break as easily."

Aloisia hugged Marcellinus and said, "Thank you." Marcellinus did nothing as he blushed.

The two left the village, waving, and were followed by much cheering and clapping from the villagers. In about two day's travel, they had come to a little forest. They cut through the trees and plants to reach the other side, when they heard men talking, along with slashes of swords cutting the trees. Marcellinus immediately recognized the language as Latin. He saw one emerge from the overgrowth, and with shocked eyes, whispered to Aloisia, "It is the Roman legionnaires. Quick, we must hide." They quickly ran as far as they could from the soldiers, and when they turned to look, they saw a large number of them pour out of the forest. Marcellinus quickly counted and said, "There are about seventy of them."

Aloisia was worried as she saw them marching towards the village of Korla and spoke. "Marcellinus, we must stop them. If they reach the village, they will more than likely take it over by force."

Marcellinus shook his head as he said, "No, there is nothing we can do. The two of us cannot defeat seventy armed soldiers. We must continue, and if we see any more, we must avoid them if we can." Aloisia looked at the soldiers and village as she weighed a heavy heart, but she knew

Marcellinus was right. As the two made their way out of the forest, they saw the rest of the encampment of soldiers resting on the bottom of the hillside. They both cautiously peeked down to notice that there were about fifty soldiers all lying around.

There were three kinds of soldiers they noticed. One type was unarmored and dressed in red shorts and shirts and carried large javelins that they probably threw from a distance. Marcellinus counted about fifteen of them. The other soldiers looked exactly like the ones that cut through the forest. It must have been the mainstay of the regime. They wore leather armor as well as red under armor. The soldiers wore a dull brass breastplate for protection. On their heads, they wore a mighty brass helmet that was adorned with three white feathers on top, each twelve inches in height, and chin straps that covered their right and left cheeks. They carried a sword and a lance as their weapons. About six of the soldiers were riding horseback. The soldiers also carried circular wooden shields that were outlined with iron. The last group of five soldiers looked like veterans. They wore a mighty iron helmet that was of the same design as the brass ones but was equipped with three blue feathers instead of white. The veteran soldiers carried a same size circular shield, but it was made completely out of iron. They also wore iron breastplates with blue under armor and carried a short sword, which was sharp, that he heard one of the soldiers call a gladius.

Marcellinus turned to speak to Aloisia. "Come, let us go around." As Marcellinus said this, a rather large man, who stood about six feet and four inches, exited one of the tents. He was dressed quite formally and looked as if he was the commander. The man had no helmet, but he wore a mighty solid silver breastplate with black-and-white-striped under armor. He also carried a long and truly mighty blade. The man then turned to show his bearded face, and Aloisia gasped as she angrily stood to her feet. Marcellinus said, "Aloisia! Get down! They will see you."

She spoke as if in another world, "That man…that is the man who killed my father!" Aloisia ran down the hill screaming and enraged. The soldiers were quickly notified of her presence and grabbed their weapons. Marcellinus, frustrated, began to follow behind her with sword in hand. As Marcellinus and Aloisia neared the bottom of the hill, they faced off with the many soldiers there. One after the other, the soldiers were cut down by the mighty blades of the warriors. Javelins flew as the unarmored soldiers chucked them at Marcellinus and Aloisia. They quickly leaped left and right to avoid the oncoming spikes. Then the six horsemen galloped towards them. Marcellinus readied his bow and arrows and, with three quick shots, killed three of the horses, knocking their riders to the ground, breaking two of the rider's necks. The other three horses rushed by Marcellinus as he gave three quick slashes while dodging the stabs of the soldiers. One after the other, the horses were all dead. Aloisia had swiftly cut through each soldier very efficiently as she neared the impressively armored man. As she got close, the five veteran soldiers began to attack her all at once.

Meanwhile, Marcellinus was locked in sword-clashing combat as he fought the many soldiers charging after him. After a while, he managed to kill all of his adversaries and then began attacking the javelin throwers. They easily fell because they carried no armor to protect them. Marcellinus looked around and saw that they had wiped out this army and that only the five veterans remained, and they were attacking Aloisia. Aloisia struggled, trying to block their sword swipes. She did manage to kill one, however. Marcellinus ran to her aid and plunged his sword deep into the side of one of the soldiers. There were now three as one broke off to fight Marcellinus. Marcellinus quickly killed the soldier in three swings of his blade. The commander unsheathed his blade and slowly approached the two warriors. Marcellinus plunged his sword into the side of one of the remaining two soldiers. As the last one stood there, shocked, Marcellinus and Aloisia both plunged their weapons deep into the man, killing him.

Then the large man approached the two and spoke in Chinese while laughing. "Very impressive. The Chinese women are very good fighters indeed. They will make great additions to the Roman Empire, or at least good bed women! Ah! Ha! Ha!" Marcellinus and Aloisia looked at him and frowned, as the man continued, "Oh, I do apologize, I forgot to introduce myself. I am Manius Lepidus. I am the praefectus castrorum, of the once mighty army that stood before you. In other words, I am the camp's prefect, the commander, if you will." Manius looked at Marcellinus and spoke. "You don't look Chinese. What are you doing here?"

Marcellinus remained silent as Aloisia screamed out, "Manius! I remember you! You murdered my father when I was a child!"

Manius grabbed his chin as he thought for a moment and then said, "Really? Hmm…it must have been from my early days when I was but a mere soldier. Sorry if I've forgotten, for I've killed so many people, it's hard to keep track of them all."

Aloisia continued, "It was when you attacked the village of Hami. You killed my father in cold blood as he tried to protect me."

Manius thought and he finally remembered, "Oh yes! I remember attacking that village. Though I'm afraid I don't remember your father. Although we were ordered not to kill any civilians, I simply couldn't help myself that day, for I can't stand the sight of you Chinese trash. So if I thought your father was ugly, then I killed him." He began to laugh hysterically, and Aloisia became enraged and began to attack Manius. Manius was indeed a skilled swordsman and he proved to be too much for Aloisia, for after a short duel, he sliced her on the arm, causing her to drop her spear. She fell, in pain, to the ground and looked up at Manius, who had raised his sword. With a maniacal smile, he began to lower it.

A tear ran down Aloisia's face while she said, "Father, I have failed you." Just as the sword was to connect with her face, another blade halted Manius's, for Marcellinus had placed his sword under Manius's, blocking it.

Manius looked up at Marcellinus as Marcellinus spoke, "That is enough."

Manius walked a few steps back as he spoke, "Oh, so you are going to fight me now, too, I see. Well, warrior, whenever you are ready."

Marcellinus readied his sword as he spoke, "I do not know of your past, nor did I see what you did to Aloisia's father. All I know is you hurt Aloisia right now, and no one touches Aloisia." Then with a mighty clash, their swords connected. A great battle ensued, with their swords clashing back and forth. They blocked left, right, up, and down. And after many swings, Manius tried to swing down to cut Marcellinus, but Marcellinus moved to the left to dodge the attack and cut Manius across the arm, causing him to drop his blade.

Manius fell to the ground while grabbing his arm. He then frantically spoke, "Wait! Don't strike me! Have mercy! I'm sorry for what I have done! Please don't kill me!"

Marcellinus looked down at the pathetic man and said, "I will not kill you." Manius looked up as Marcellinus continued, "But she will." As he said this, Aloisia dug her spear deep into the side of Manius. Manius grunted in pain as blood came out of his wound. He now lay on the ground, dead and motionless. Marcellinus looked at the crying Aloisia and said, "Come. We must make haste, for the rest of the army might return soon."

They both traveled for three more days and nights and reached the next village of their journey. The village they came to was called Dunhuang.

# Chapter 24

The village of Dunhuang was quite peaceful. Marcellinus and Aloisia stopped at an inn for the night. Marcellinus spoke to Aloisia. "I only purchased one room for both of us to share, is…is that all right?"

Aloisia seemed a bit surprised as she nodded and said, "Yes, it is fine." They made their way to the room and put their sacks down upon the floor.

Marcellinus spoke to Aloisia before she took off her armor. "Aloisia, are you doing all right?" He approached her as he continued, "You did it back there. You were truly amazing. Your father would be very proud of you."

Aloisia wiped her tears as she hugged Marcellinus and said, "Thank you, Marcellinus. You saved my life again. I have never had as good of a friend as you before. Thank you for staying by me."

Marcellinus helped her sit down on the bed as they sat side by side. He grabbed her face and made it point towards his face and spoke, "Aloisia, you are welcome. I will always be there for you." He looked down towards the ground as he swallowed a large lump of saliva, building up his courage, and said, "Actually, Aloisia, I have something to say to you. I have wanted to say it for a long time now, but I never really knew how to say it or if it was appropriate. My father has always taught me to follow my heart, and my heart is telling me this is the right thing to do so…" He hesitated a bit but continued, "Aloisia, I know I must marry Princess Nangong, but the truth is, I am in love with you. I have loved you for a very long time now. I no longer care about what the emperor's orders were. I just want to go home to my father and live my life with you by my side forever. I want to start a family with you. I want to make love to you. I want to be the best husband to you that I can possibly be. I know this is really shocking but…"

Then Aloisia made Marcellinus halt his speech as she placed her finger upon his lips and said, "Shh…you talk too much." She smiled and blushed as she said, "I'm so glad to hear you say this, for I have been in love with you since the day we met." They looked at each other with loving eyes as they reached in for a kiss. They soon found themselves embraced in each other's arms as they began to make love on the bed.

They both awoke the next morning, naked and in each other's arms. Marcellinus and Aloisia gave each other a kiss as they said good morning to each other. They stood and put their clothes back on. Marcellinus and Aloisia walked outside and began their journey back to Marcellinus's home. Marcellinus held Aloisia's hand as he said, "Come. Let us go home."

They exited Dunhuang and had only traveled for one day and night when they approached a large, grassy plain. The sky began to grow dark and the clouds eclipsed the sun as thunder boomed in the sky. Then a loud and angry voice was heard. "Marcellinus!"

They both recognized the voice from earlier and said, "It is the demon!" The ground began to shake like an earthquake as the two stepped back. Then the ground split in two to reveal a large lake of boiling hot magma. The hole stretched for a good ten tree lengths. Suddenly, a massive beast came bursting through the lava and stood ferociously tall while lightning was striking all around.

The creature was quite a sight to behold indeed. Only half of the beast's body was seen, as its lower half was still submerged in the lava. Only having half of the body visible, it still stood an incredible twenty tree lengths tall. As they got a better look at the goliath, they noticed it was a large and mighty dragon. The entire body was covered in sharp, pointy spikes protruding forth. Under the belly it showed lines separating body segments, which were a dark yellow color. The scaly skin was a dark red crimson color. All along the back and sides of its neck, the beast had long, sharp, deadly looking horns, which were each about half a tree length long. The horns got longer and thicker as they stretched down its back. The dragon was adorned with titanic wings that stretched longer than the whole body, at about twenty-five tree lengths long. The muscular wings were equipped with tiny spikes that stretched across the appendage, which were separated by orange-colored skin membranes. The two visible arms were quite beefy and were also covered with spines. It had three long fingers, each adorned with twelve inch blades. The face was indeed gruesome as the monster opened its mouth, revealing two rows of sharp teeth that were five inches long each. The eyes glowed with a fearsome bloody red color as it slipped its forked tongue in and out, hissing and growling. The beast also had two large, thick demonic horns atop its head, which were at least five tree lengths long. There was also a row of spikes below its chin.

The behemoth spoke after giving a thunderous roar. "Marcellinus and Aloisia! You shall both be destroyed!"

Marcellinus looked up at the colossal demon and spoke. "Why do you want to kill me, demon?"

The dragon roared as it spoke, "How dare you, a mere human, address me in such a manner! I am Iblis! The king of the underworld!" The beast continued, "You have destroyed my servants, and so I have come to seek your life! My gargoyles and phoenix were sent here by me to cleanse this world of human filth! They had helped to awaken ancient beasts to help me kill the humans. You came along and killed every one of them! One after another! Not even Mogui or Kemaila could stop you."

Marcellinus spoke. "Why do you wish to kill the humans?"

Iblis continued, "Why should I explain myself to you? Though if you really want to know, then allow me to grant your final wish. I wish to rule this world, and you humans are contaminating it, so you must be eliminated!" Then, with a mighty slash, the dragon swooped his hand down. Marcellinus and Aloisia barely missed being slashed as they rolled to safety. The beast breathed fire and nearly burned Marcellinus. Marcellinus rose to his feet from rolling and fired many arrows from his bow. The arrows did little to no damage at all, and the demon laughed and said, "Your pathetic arrows are no match for me!" Marcellinus began to throw his knives at the beast. They struck the hide of the titanic demon as it screamed in pain. Marcellinus knew that the beast could indeed be destroyed. Iblis became enraged as he spewed mighty balls of fire at Marcellinus. Aloisia was in the back and stood watching, knowing there was nothing she could really do, for the beast was in the middle of searing hot lava and she had nothing to throw. If she threw her spear, then that would leave her unarmed if the blow to the dragon was not fatal. Marcellinus continued tossing knives until he finally noticed he had run out. Iblis laughed and said, "You have run out of knives. Now what will you do, pest?" Marcellinus knew he had to somehow reach the beast's heart and kill it once and for all, but how? It was sitting in the middle of a lakebed of lava. Marcellinus realized what he had to do. He dodged flames until Iblis smashed his massive hand on the ground. When he did, Marcellinus hopped upon his extended arm. Like lightning, Marcellinus ran up the arm to approach his chest. Iblis blew fire down at Marcellinus as he raised his arm.

Marcellinus made a super human leap towards the beast's chest and screamed, "Go to hell, demon!" He plunged his sword deep into the heart of Iblis. The beast screamed and wriggled in pain. Aloisia saw this happening and quickly pulled some rope from her sack. She tied a knot around her spear and threw it in Marcellinus's direction as he was hanging on to the handle of his sword, slowly losing his grip. It delved deep into Iblis, making a makeshift zip line. Marcellinus grabbed the rope and slid down to the safety of the ground.

As Marcellinus grabbed Aloisia in comfort, they heard the beast scream in his final moments, "No! How could I be defeated by a mere human! This can't be!" And with a mighty explosion of bright light, the demon was no more. Marcellinus and Aloisia watched as the clouds disappeared from in front of the sun and the ground shifted back to normal. The day was beautiful and peaceful once more. They hugged and kissed each other as a ray of sunshine shined down upon them. The two began their journey home once more.

# Chapter 25

In fifteen days and nights, they finally reached the border of Chang'an. Marcellinus and Aloisia approached the border gates as the guard spoke, "Halt! Who goes there?"

Marcellinus spoke, "It is I, Marcellinus. And this is my friend Aloisia, we have traveled together and completed the emperor's request."

The guard looked shocked as he spoke out loud, "What? Marcellinus? You…you have returned?" He gave the signal to open the gates. As they walked through the mighty doors, the guardsman approached him, saying, "Nobody in Chang'an thought we'd ever see you again! How was your journey? Did you face many obstacles?"

Marcellinus spoke hastily, "I shall tell the details of my journey to the emperor. If you wish to hear it, then please come to the palace." The guardsman nodded. Marcellinus looked around as he spoke once more, "How is my father, Hototo, doing?"

The guardsman looked at Marcellinus with troubled eyes as he spoke. "Hototo was very depressed when you left. He sold his armor and got the coins he needed for the herbs. Hototo's doing fine now, but he hardly makes himself public since you left two-and-a-half years ago."

Marcellinus gasped in amazement as he said, "Two-and-a-half years? I have been gone that long?" The guardsman nodded. Marcellinus must have lost track of time; he was amazed to hear that he was gone for so long. He looked at Aloisia and spoke. "Aloisia, have we really been gone for two-and-a-half years?"

Aloisia looked shocked as well as she said, "I guess so, but it surely didn't seem that long. I wonder how my family is doing, having been without me for so long." Marcellinus waved to the guardsman as the two ran quickly towards Hototo's house.

They reached the home in no time to notice no sign of Hototo anywhere. As Marcellinus ran inside, Aloisia stayed outside. She began to marvel at how cute and quaint the house was. Marcellinus burst through the door and began shouting, "Father! Father! It is I, Marcellinus! Where are you, Father?"

Then an elderly voice spoke out as Hototo entered the room, "Marcellinus? Is that you, my son?" Marcellinus smiled as he ran to hug his father. Hototo began to cry as he hugged his son. Then Hototo spoke, "My son. I worried for you every day you were gone. How was your journey? Did you make it to Syria?"

Marcellinus pulled the necklace from his bag to show Hototo as he said, "Yes, I did. I am sorry it took so long to complete my journey, but look at this, Father. It is a necklace from Alexander the Great, given to me as a reward in Syria."

Hototo looked confused as he asked, "What do you mean, a reward, my son?" Marcellinus began to tell Hototo his entire story of his journey, how he slew many monsters and demons, and described what each one looked like. He described the many different villages and people he saw, and of course, he spoke the most about Aloisia and how he fell in love. Hototo gasped to hear of such a marvelous tale full of danger and excitement. He spoke. "My son. You have truly made me proud." Marcellinus told Hototo to come with him outside. Hototo was introduced to Aloisia, who was still standing there, waiting.

Aloisia spoke as she shook Hototo's hand with a smile. "Hello, you must be Marcellinus's father. I'm Aloisia. I've heard so much about you."

Hototo was speechless as he saw how beautiful Aloisia really was. Hototo finally said, "The pleasure is all mine. Thank you for helping my son complete his quest." She just smiled. Hototo turned to speak to Marcellinus and said, "I know you love Aloisia, but what of Princess Nangong? The emperor will be most displeased."

Marcellinus spoke to Hototo, "Well, Father, I will just have to decline the arrangement, for I am in love with Aloisia, and I want to be with her forever."

Hototo smiled as he said, "This will shock the emperor very much. Then again, we could get lucky and he might have a heart attack seeing you alive." The three of them laughed as they walked towards the palace.

When they entered the city, all the citizens of Chang'an stared in amazement and stood with gaping mouths, pointing at Marcellinus. Soon they approached the palace, and a guard quickly noticed Marcellinus. He ran inside to retrieve the emperor. Emperor Wu was enjoying some tea with Princess Nangong as the guard came rushing in to say, "Emperor Wu, your majesty! The Xirong, Marcellinus has returned!"

Emperor Wu dropped his tea cup as he said, "Impossible!" He stumbled to his feet to make his way outside, with the princess closely behind. The emperor stepped outside and saw that it was indeed true. Marcellinus, Hototo, and Aloisia all bowed to their knees in front of the emperor as all of Chang'an stood to watch. The emperor stood there for a moment, quite stunned, but then he spoke out, "I see you have made it back, Marcellinus. Have you brought proof of your journey?"

Marcellinus grabbed the necklace as he placed it in front of the emperor and said, "This is a necklace of Alexander the Great. It was given to me in Syria by a Roman man."

Emperor Wu picked up the necklace as he stared in awe at its splendor, for he had never seen such a thing before. Then he stared at his many subjects as he whispered to Nangong, "What should I do, sister? I never expected the Xirong to survive the quest."

Nangong looked just as shocked as the emperor did as she said, "I don't know, brother. But perhaps you should keep your word? I guess I have to marry the Xirong now. Thanks a lot, brother."

Emperor Wu hesitated a bit and then, as he licked his lips in nervousness and anger, spoke forth, "Marcellinus, since you have completed your journey, I shall keep true to my word. First, can you tell me what you encountered on your journey? Were there really demons and monsters?"

Marcellinus rose to his feet and turned to face the citizens of Chang'an, and he spoke of his adventure. He spoke on how he and Aloisia fought many monsters and demons. Marcellinus explained what each one looked like and how vigorous the battles were. He talked about the many different people and villages.

Marcellinus turned to Emperor Wu and spoke to him about the port in Syria and how he could trade to Europe by ship. Emperor Wu was most pleased and he spoke with a smile. "Very well, Marcellinus. I hereby grant you a mountain of gold and my sister's hand in marriage."

The entire city began to scream and holler in excitement. Marcellinus turned to the saddened face of Aloisia, and with great boldness, he spoke forth, "I am sorry, Emperor Wu, for I cannot marry Princess Nangong." He turned to Aloisia with a smile, as she smiled back, and continued, "I am in love with another beautiful woman." Emperor Wu, and the entire city, was shocked, as this was unheard of. No one ever disobeyed the emperor's orders.

Emperor Wu became outraged as he yelled, "How dare you disobey my orders, Xirong! My word is law. If I say you must marry my sister, then you must marry her!"

Marcellinus looked at the emperor with a frown and said, "No. I cannot. And I will not."

Emperor Wu was now blinded by rage as he said, "Guards! Seize that Xirong!" Then four guards grabbed Marcellinus by the arms as the emperor continued, "Take this fool out back and dispose of him!"

While the guards were walking away, Hototo gained his courage and spoke out of line. "Wait!" Emperor Wu and the guards looked at Hototo with shock as Hototo continued, "Emperor Wu, I, Hototo Takeshi, have always been your loyal servant. I have brought you medicine on several occasions, and my ancestors had the utmost respect for your great-grandfather and grandfather. What you are doing is wrong, your highness! Marcellinus may be just a Xirong to you, but he has done nothing but follow your orders. For two-and-a-half years, my son has risked his life to complete his journey, a journey you sent him on! He has destroyed many monsters and demons on your behalf! Now because he refuses to marry Princess Nangong, you are going to kill him?" He turned to face the citizens as he continued, "If this is how Emperor Wu treats a man who has completed a difficult journey for him, then I don't want to imagine how he'll treat you, the citizens of Chang'an!"

Emperor Wu began to sweat as he looked upon the now angry citizens of Chang'an. They were screaming, "Let Marcellinus go!" and "He has done nothing wrong. Let him go!" Emperor Wu knew that the last thing he wanted was a rebellion, as they would surely try to overthrow him.

Emperor Wu raised his hands in the air and said, "Enough! Very well, if you want the Xirong to live, then so be it."

He ordered the guards to release him, and Marcellinus walked to his father and hugged him, saying, "Thank you, Father. Thank you for saving me."

Hototo hugged him back and spoke, "Nothing is more important than you, my son."

They turned to face Emperor Wu as the Emperor said, "You may still have the gold, Xirong, and you can marry whomever you want. But you are never allowed to enter Chang'an again! Not you, Hototo, or that girl who's with you!" Then he continued as he charged back into his palace, "Now take your gold and go!" Marcellinus, Aloisia, and Hototo grabbed every bit of gold that the emperor gave them and left the city.

On their way back home, they purchased four horses with their newfound riches. Once they got home, the three of them tied the horses down and entered the house. They sat down together and began to discuss what they wanted to do. Hototo seemed like he wanted to stay at his house. Marcellinus saw from Aloisia's facial expression that she missed her family when they were talking about living at Hototo's house. Marcellinus was feeling helpless and under pressure, for he knew not what to do. Should he stay at Hototo's house and have Aloisia be sad? Or should he live at Aloisia's house and have Hototo be sad? Marcellinus could not bear to be separated from either one of them. Not wanting to see either one sad, Marcellinus spoke to Hototo hesitantly. "Father, I must return with Aloisia to the city of Hami so she can be reunited with her family. I would be honored if you would come with me, Father, for there is nothing left for you here. Emperor Wu has banished you from the city, and you can no longer make a living here. Using our riches, we can buy a great house and live there together. Aloisia and I can then, perhaps, start a family."

Hototo smiled and said, "I do not mind leaving here as long as I am with you, my son. I am happy no matter where I go." They smiled and began packing all the belongings that they could into bags and sacks to put on the horses. They walked outside to leave and loaded the fourth horse with as much as it could carry and then left their home forever. Marcellinus and Hototo turned to look at their house, as if to say good-bye, and turned once more and began galloping to the border gates.

As they got to the gates, the guardsman approached them and said he was sorry that they had to leave the city and never return. The guardsman spoke. "Where will you go now?"

Marcellinus looked at Aloisia and held her hand, saying, "We are going to Hami to settle down and start a family."

The guardsman smiled as he signaled for the gate to be opened, and as Marcellinus rode by, the guardsman spoke. "I wish you luck in starting your new family, Marcellinus!" Then Marcellinus, Aloisia, and Hototo rode off into the grassy fields as the sun set behind them in a beautiful orange and red glow. For it was the beginning of a whole new life for them, and Marcellinus would always be remembered by the city of Chang'an as the Silk Road Warrior.

# EPILOGUE

After Marcellinus had completed his journey, Emperor Wu ordered General Zhang Qian to journey the same path as Marcellinus, in the year 138 BC. When General Qian returned with the good news of a safe travel, Emperor Wu declared the path to be named the Silk Road. Emperor Wu would later die of old age in the year 86 BC, almost immediately after the famed witchcraft trials.

Princess Nangong continued to live as royalty for the rest of her life. She eventually claimed her own city and ruled there. However, it is unknown whether she married or not.

The Romans continued their quest of pillaging, and eventually they conquered many towns. Fortunately, they were all far away from Marcellinus and Aloisia.

The monsters and demons never appeared again, and many people forgot about them as they faded from reality into myth.

As for Marcellinus, Aloisia, and Hototo, they moved back to Aloisia's town of Hami. She reunited with her family once more, and in less than a month, she married Marcellinus. Marcellinus used his gold to build a massive house adorned with many fancy things near Aloisia's family in Hami. Marcellinus and Aloisia lived there with Hototo for many wonderful years. Aloisia gave birth to three beautiful children, two boys and one girl. Hototo lived to see the third grandchild born; he then died a month later. Marcellinus and Aloisia died at a very old age, and each one of their children became parents as well. It is unknown if Marcellinus ever again saw the villagers he had once saved. Aloisia and Marcellinus's legacy would live on in the village of Hami for all time.